THE LAST ALOHA

MAUI ISLAND SERIES BOOK 4

KELLIE COATES GILBERT

Copyright © 2022 by Kellie Coates Gilbert

All rights reserved.

No part of this book may be reproduced in any form or by any electronic or mechanical means, including information storage and retrieval systems, without written permission from the author, except for the use of brief quotations in a book review.

The Last Aloha is a work of fiction. Names, characters, places, and incidents are either the product of the author's imagination or are used fictitiously, and any resemblance to actual persons, living or dead, is coincidental.

Cover design: Elizabeth Mackay

*For my husband, Allen.
On this tenth anniversary of my publishing career, you continue to support me in every way. I could not have become a full-time author without you by my side. I love you.*

PRAISE FOR KELLIE'S BOOKS

"If you're looking for a new author to read, you can't go wrong with Kellie Coates Gilbert."
~**Lisa Wingate**, NY Times bestselling author of *Before We Were Yours*

"Well-drawn, sympathetic characters and graceful language"
~**Library Journal**

"Deft, crisp storytelling"
~**RT Book Reviews**

"I devoured the book in one sitting."
~**Chick Lit Central**

"Gilbert's heartfelt fiction is always a pleasure to read."
~**Buzzing About Books**

"Kellie Coates Gilbert delivers emotionally gripping plots and authentic characters."
~**Life Is Story**

"I laughed, I cried, I wanted to throw my book against the wall, but I couldn't quit reading."
    ~**Amazon reader**

"I have read other books I had a hard time putting down, but this story totally captivated me."
    ~**Goodreads reader**

"I became somewhat depressed when the story actually ended. I wanted more."
    ~**Barnes and Noble reader**

ALSO BY KELLIE COATES GILBERT

THE MAUI ISLAND SERIES

Under The Maui Sky

Silver Island Moon

Tides of Paradise

The Last Aloha

Ohana Sunrise

THE PACIFIC BAY SERIES

Chances Are

Remember Us

Chasing Wind

Between Rains

THE SUN VALLEY SERIES

Sisters

Heartbeats

Changes

Promises

LOVE ON VACATION SERIES

Otherwise Engaged

All Fore Love

TEXAS GOLD SERIES

A Woman of Fortune

Where Rivers Part

A Reason to Stay

What Matters Most

STAND ALONE NOVELS

Mother of Pearl

Available at all retailers

www.kelliecoatesgilbert.com

THE LAST ALOHA
MAUI ISLAND SERIES, BOOK 4

Kellie Coates Gilbert

1

A loud wail woke Shane Briscoe out of a dead sleep. Exhausted, he bolted up, wiped his eyes, then clambered from the tangled sheets and raced in the direction of the cries.

Carson's room was located down the hall from his own. In his hurry, Shane stubbed his toe on the doorjamb and let out a thundering—and very colorful—string of curse words before he remembered little ears were nearby. The upside? The powerful sound of his voice stopped the baby's cries.

Shane flicked on the light and shielded his eyes from the brightness with his forearm placed across his face. He stumbled to the crib against the wall and stepped on a rattle that had been left on the floor from their playtime together the night before. "Fu...dge!" he yelled, pausing mid-word to alter what he'd intended to say.

Carson whimpered and Shane lifted him, bringing his warm little body against his own. Immediately, wetness seeped onto his arm.

Shane groaned and headed for the changing table where he expertly unsnapped the lower part of the onesie with one hand, took hold of Carson's little ankles with the other and lifted him up. With a deft and swift maneuver, Shane released the tiny bottom from the soaked diaper and tossed the sopping thing in the nearby can, letting the lid drop with a thud. His hand reached for the shelf on the wall and pulled down a clean diaper from the stack. In the process, he toppled the entire bunch. Disposable diapers cascaded down on his baby's head.

Shane waited for his son's renewed wails. Hearing none, he looked down. Carson's face broke into an adorable grin, as if his little boy thought his dad's clumsy antics were funny.

Shane finished diapering Carson, then lifted him from the table. He nuzzled his nose against his baby's neck, taking in the powdery, sweet smell. "You hungry, little man?"

He wandered with his son into the kitchen, the beautiful kitchen with white cabinetry and a spacious island topped with granite—the kitchen meant for Aimee. The moment she'd seen the double-door refrigerator, the gas stove with the fancy vent top...well, she'd gone nuts. She wouldn't even look at another house.

"This is the one," she'd exclaimed, clasping her hands in front of her chest like all her prayers had come true. Little had either of them known that Aimee would not cook a single meal in this new kitchen.

Instead, she'd left a note. A stupid note. An impersonal scrap of paper that had broken his heart and dashed his dreams of being a family. She didn't even have the decency to tell him face-to-face that she was walking out on their engagement...and their son.

Shane didn't know what he'd wrestled with more...anger or the deep hurt. Both, he supposed. It hadn't gotten a whole lot better in the months since she'd hightailed it back to Los Angeles to follow her wacky dream of becoming a star.

"I want to be somebody," she often claimed. Apparently, being a wife and a mother meant nothing to her.

Shane shook his head as he warmed Carson's bottle. Fame must mean a lot if someone is willing to swap their soul to get it.

He wandered into the living room, carrying his baby son and the bottle. The room had a single sofa. That was it...oh, except for the television mounted to the wall. Despite his skinny finances, if he was going to spend nights rocking a baby, he was at least going to enjoy some screen time.

He plopped onto the plush cushions, pulled a sofa blanket over the two of them, and poised the bottle in front of his baby's mouth. "You ready, buddy? Chow time."

Carson latched onto the bottle and ate hungrily until the formula was nearly gone. Among lots of other things, Shane still had to remind himself to pull the nipple from that tiny mouth every so often and burp Carson to keep his little tummy from cramping up.

Seconds later, Carson rewarded the effort with a loud, infant-sized belch.

"Atta boy," Shane said, pulling the baby back down to his lap. He repositioned the bottle into his son's mouth.

Shane leaned his head against the cushion and closed his eyes. He was nearly asleep when he felt something on his arm.

He slowly opened his eyes. Carson smiled back at him and stroked Shane with his tiny, dimpled hand.

AVA BRISCOE PULLED the belt on her robe a little tighter and wandered to her kitchen window. She peered out at the worker shanties in the distance. Christel claimed she was overprotective of her youngest, but she liked knowing Shane was only a few hundred yards from her own front door, especially when he was hurting. Now, he and her new grandson lived in Napili-Honokowai, north of the Kaanapali beach area.

The entire family was still reeling from Aimee's decision to bail from her wedding to Shane. Worse? She'd deserted her son. How could a woman do that?

Ava shook her head in disgust. She would never understand how people could callously hurt the ones they said they loved.

As she moved to the cupboard for a teacup, something out the window caught her attention. She returned to the sink and leaned forward, trying to make out what she'd seen. In seconds, a figure stepped into the light cast from the yard pole.

Wimberly Ann Jenkins!

Ava's breath caught. She watched as Mig took hold of Wimberly Ann's elbow and guided her to her car. He opened the door.

Before Wimberly Ann climbed in, Mig pulled her close. He kissed her. The kiss was long, lasting far longer than Ava felt comfortable watching. Still, she couldn't seem to look away.

It seemed her faithful operations manager had fallen for the new realtor, a gal who resembled Dolly Parton—a woman who had been married six times!

Miguel Nakamoto was a fixture here at Pali Maui, having worked at the pineapple plantation longer than anyone—nearly as long as Ava. His responsibilities included managing the fields and the packing operation, and supervising the employees. He was good at his job and highly respected. Ava was grateful to work alongside him, especially now that her husband had passed away.

Certainly, Mig had been alone for a long time. In a story that nearly duplicated Shane's, Mig's wife, who the entire family had nicknamed the "Plate Thrower," left with another man when their daughter, Leilani, was only eleven.

After all these years, Ava had assumed Mig had determined he would remain a single man—a decision that was entirely understandable, given what he'd experienced.

Then Wimberly Ann arrived on the scene. In no time, Mig

started acting like a smitten teenager. Ava noticed he wore cologne, even out in the fields. He urged Katie to take him shopping for some new clothes, and not just any clothes. According to their shared housekeeper, he'd tossed his work shirts and pants in the back of his closet. Mig was now wearing Rhoback polos and Tommy Bahama half-zip pullovers—in a shade of coral, no less!

At Wimberly Ann's suggestion, he made an appointment with a stylist in Wailea and had his straight-cut jet-black hair fashioned into a side part with a quiff. Wimberly Ann claimed the cut played up his thick hair.

Ava shook her head. She wanted to tell him to be careful.

Love might be heaven, but could quickly turn to pure hell.

2

Christel Briscoe raised her leg from the sudsy water and ran a razor across her skin. She did the same with her other leg, then stepped from the sunken tub and wrapped a thick white towel around her body and moved for the hook where her bathrobe hung.

She was going out tonight—a special date with her favorite guy, Dr. Evan Matisse.

Christel met Evan nearly a year ago, only a short time after her father died. On the heels of learning of her dad's betrayal with a family friend, her brother Aiden was in a boating accident that left him with severe, life-threatening, injuries. He came through it all, largely because of Dr. Matisse.

The attraction had been nearly instant. Christel remembered how grateful she'd been that Evan had brought Aiden out of danger. In the hospital waiting room, she'd flung her arms around his neck in gratitude.

There was instantly a spark as she felt his chest against her own, as she smelled his cologne and took in the way he'd smiled back at her. He was smitten as well, she could tell. Or, at least she had hoped.

Oh, she didn't admit any of that to herself, or to anyone else, for some time. Her heart was still in a sling after being broken. She'd been forced to divorce her first husband, her first love, Jay, when his addiction got out of control. His life spiraled down, and he took her with him.

There were countless nights spent on the phone at four in the morning, checking with the police and the local hospital to see if he had been in an accident when he failed to come home. There were overdrawn bank accounts, sometimes to the tune of thousands of dollars. She'd work to cover the deficits, but could never cover the hit to her credit score. Her gut twisted each time he pulled into their driveway as she wondered if he would be able to walk to the door without her help.

Eventually, she could no longer deny the toll to her health and emotional wellbeing. She could no longer bear the shame.

It hadn't always been that way, of course. There was a time, early in their marriage, when they were deeply in love. Jay was fun and supportive. He made her laugh. Jay had a unique way of making her believe she could fly to the moon and back. He was her entire world, and she was his.

Christel turned her concentration to what she was going to wear. She sifted through the garments in her closet, finally choosing a black dress she bought last year and had never worn. The dress would look great with her dainty diamond pendant. Satisfied with her selection, she moved to get dressed while thoughts of her marriage continued to linger.

It pained her still, thinking about all they had lost. Addiction was like that. It snuck in the door and stole everything valuable, never looking back. Never caring that you were puddled on the floor, devastated and in tears. Never worrying about the shame, or what the future would bring and how chemical abuse could cause you to lose your job, your health, and finally, your relationships.

Despite the hurt, Christel was proud of herself for untethering from the hurricane that had become her life. She'd bravely chosen to become emotionally well again. She'd quit enabling, and started living.

Now, things were completely different. Evan was completely different.

He'd had his own hardship. His beloved fiancé had been killed in a helicopter accident while serving in the Middle East. The loss of both the woman he'd loved and his unborn child had nearly broken him.

Together, Evan and Christel had taken hold of each other's hands and risked their hearts again. Even if a little. They both agreed to take things slow. There was no need to rush. If real, they wanted their love to have time to develop and mature. They weren't lovesick teens. They were two adults hoping to commit for life to a person they adored—someone who could be fully trusted.

Eventually, she had to admit her heart had been captured by this wonderful man—a guy who was incredibly smart, funny, and most of all, kind. Evan was someone who would be there by her side. He could be counted on and would do anything for her. He'd even carry her off a mountainside, if necessary. Surprisingly, he had done just that when she injured her ankle.

His strong arms underneath her made her feel safe and secure...loved.

Christel wasn't sure she would ever feel like that again. Did true love really come around twice? She was starting to believe that it did.

Christel pulled her favorite bracelet into place when her doorbell rang. She smiled in anticipation and headed for the living room to answer it.

On the other side of her front door stood Evan wearing a suit and tie.

"Boy, you weren't kidding when you said to dress up," she said, thankful she'd donned a party dress—a black sheath with a ruffle at the bottom hem made of chiffon. It was simple, yet appropriately elegant.

Evan leaned and kissed her cheek.

"You look stunning," he told her as he moved for her neck.

She giggled and gently pushed him back. "Later," she scolded. "We have dinner reservations. If we get *that* started, we'll most certainly be late." She winked.

On second thought, who cared? She wouldn't mind him unzipping that little black dress of hers.

From the look on his face, Evan was thinking the same.

Putting their amorous impulses on hold, Christel grabbed her purse and Evan led her out to his car.

"I have a surprise," Evan said, his expression much like a kid at Christmas.

Christel clicked her seatbelt into place. "You know I don't like surprises."

"You'll like this one." Evan started the engine and pulled out. "And don't even try to guess. You'll never figure it out."

"Never?" Her face pulled into a serious look, ready to take on the challenge. "Are you sure of that?"

She spent the next minutes quizzing him. Did the surprise include where they were having dinner?

"Maybe," he teased. "But that's not the main surprise."

She scowled. "Is your big surprise a someone?"

Evan shook his head, grinning. "Nope." He reached and took her hand in his own, gently squeezing. "Don't even try. I promise you will not land on the correct answer."

She didn't, of course—until he pulled his car into the airport. She glanced over at him with her eyebrows lifted. "We're picking someone up?"

"I already told you my surprise was not a person. It's much

better." He seemed unable to hold in his excitement a moment longer. "We're taking a little trip."

Christel pulled her hand from his. "But I didn't pack. I need—"

He didn't let her finish. "Don't worry, we'll be back later tonight."

Their destination did not become known until Evan led her to the ticket counter. He pulled two printed receipts and handed them to the lady who stood ready to help them. "Two roundtrips for Honolulu, please."

"Yes, sir." The woman pressed several spots on her monitor which prompted the printing of two plane tickets. She handed them over. "Have a nice flight."

Evan took Christel's hand. "Ready?"

She cocked her head, puzzled. "That's the surprise? What's in Honolulu?"

"You'll see," he told her as he led her down the skywalk.

The flight from Maui to Honolulu took just under an hour. Upon finding a waiting town car ready to transport them to their destination, Christel turned to Evan. "You are full of surprises, tonight," she remarked, as she nodded to the chauffeur and climbed into the back seat.

"The best is still ahead," Evan promised. "I hope you're hungry."

"Famished." She hadn't eaten much at all the entire day. The tiny bowl of raspberries she'd enjoyed for breakfast had been hours ago. Once she got to work, she couldn't seem to catch a long enough break to get lunch.

Her busy work days had just gotten a lot more hectic. After much contemplation, the family had made a decision to move forward with renovating and expanding the golf course at Pali Maui. Much of the work to finance the project had fallen to her, of course.

Evan slipped his hand over hers as they made their way from the airport and headed in the direction of the towering buildings filling the skyline. Oahu and Maui were decidedly different, with Oahu being far more cosmopolitan and crowded, especially Honolulu. While she didn't travel here often, Christel had enjoyed feeling in the middle of corporate America again each time she attended meetings around long granite tables with shippers, advertising agencies, and regulatory officials.

Christel decided to try again for some hint of what was ahead.

"So, Evan. Where are we going?" she asked, using her most convincing voice. Unlike most women, she didn't care for surprises. She liked the opportunity to plan and prepare for whatever was to come.

Evan quickly shut down her effort.

"You'll see." He patted her hand and grinned back at her.

Twenty minutes later, their destination was finally revealed when the chauffeur pulled the town car to a stop in front of the entrance to 53 by the Sea, a trendy and very exclusive restaurant located on the edge of the water.

"We're here," Evan announced.

"Oh, my goodness! How in the world did you ever get reservations? The waiting list for 53 by the Sea is often months out."

Evan winked. "I have my ways."

Inside, a grand staircase with wrought-iron railings led to a chic glass-walled dining room provided breathtaking views of the Kewalo Basin Harbor. Only last month, Christel had seen a magazine article touting the establishment as "the best Hawaii has to offer."

A maître d' guided them to a linen-draped table with tiny candles and rare, white hibiscus blooms arranged in the center. Christel slipped into her chair feeling a bit like Cinderella.

"Evan, this is amazing," she said as she placed her linen napkin across her lap. A waiter then took their order.

Their first course was caviar-topped toast points served with crème fraîche, minced egg, topped with chives. The appetizer paired beautifully with Old-Fashioned cocktails made with smoked bourbon infused with lemon and honey and served with a sprig of fresh rosemary and a large maraschino cherry.

The next course was French onion soup. Christel couldn't begin to eat all of the gooey gouda cheese melted on top. Salads followed, delicate plates with hearts of palm sprinkled with toasted almonds and a reduction of raspberry balsamic vinegar drizzled over top.

Evan chose a prime New York strip for his main course. The steak was served with roasted maitake mushrooms, grilled asparagus, and a purée of truffle roasted cauliflower. She selected the seared scallops with poached pear and pickled shitake mushrooms.

When they'd finished, they let their dinner settle. Evan ran his finger along Christel's bare arm. His expression changed, growing serious. "I have another surprise."

Another surprise? Christel could barely keep up with this man.

Before she could respond, he reached in his suit pocket and pulled out a tiny velvet box. He held it in the air for only a moment, then slid it across the table until it rested before her.

Christel's heart skipped a beat. Her ears began ringing and her hands grew clammy as she slowly reached for the box. "What—what is this?"

"Open it," he urged.

She lifted the box from the table and slowly raised the lid. Inside, a solitaire diamond ring in a beautiful emerald cut twinkled in the candlelight. The stone had to be at least two carats.

Christel flushed. "This is a diamond."

The corners of Evan's eyes crinkled as he smiled back at her. "Correct."

"But...why? I mean, you're giving me a diamond." Finding it suddenly hard to breathe, she set the little box on the table and stared at the ring.

Evan glanced around and gave a slight nod. Suddenly, a violinist appeared at their table. The gentleman lifted his instrument and began playing the most beautiful rendition of "To Make You Feel My Love," a song she'd long adored ever since she heard it played at a Bob Dylan concert when she was in high school.

Evan folded to one knee in front of her and took both her hands in his. "Christel, there was a time after losing Tess that I was sure I'd never be in love again." He looked deeply into her eyes. "I was wrong."

Christel felt tears sprout. She swallowed.

"I love you, Christel. And I want to marry you. Will you be my wife?" He said the words quietly, and waited.

Christel never thought she could love again after Jon. They certainly had that in common. Evan had changed all that. He was everything she needed, all she could possibly want in a life partner. She loved him. "Yes, Evan. I'll marry you."

She could barely breathe as the words came out of her mouth. This was a huge step, one she had not been prepared to make. She had not seen his proposal coming. Yet truly, there was no other answer she could possibly entertain. Of course, she'd marry him.

Christel flung her arms around Evan's neck, now openly crying. "Yes! I'll marry you."

Suddenly, several wait staff appeared. One carried a cake covered in sparklers. Another held a silver bucket with ice and champagne nestled deep within. Yet another carried a dozen red roses and laid them in Christel's arms.

"I can't believe you did all this," she exclaimed. "Without me even suspecting."

When they'd finished the impromptu celebration, Evan took her hand and they left the restaurant. As they reached the waiting town car, Evan bent and removed his shoes and socks.

"What are you doing?" Christel asked. Nothing would surprise her now.

Evan laughed. "Take your shoes off. We're going for a walk on the beach."

"At this hour? Evan, it's nearly midnight."

Evan told her to quit arguing and go with the flow. He didn't want the night to be over. Not yet.

As they reached the edge of the sand, he wove his fingers with hers. "The surprises are over," he told her. "Now, you get to plan the ceremony. Anything you want. I'm in. Spare no cost."

Christel grew pensive. Her first wedding had been spectacular. She went all out. Her mother, with the help of Alani, attended to every detail. She and Jon were wed at Wailea Chapel with Elta officiating. She had four bridesmaids. Jon had an equal number of groomsmen. Christel wore a custom Vera Wang gown, simple and elegant, and had carried a spray of lilies of the valley. On her special day, she'd felt like a princess walking the aisle with Jon waiting at the end, tears streaming down his face.

While magical, Christel wasn't sure she really wanted all that again. Not after how her first marriage ended.

"Evan, all this is very new to me. I'm still letting all of what happened tonight sink in. I do know I don't want a big ceremony. Is that okay with you?" Then, she remembered Evan was engaged to Tess and they'd never had the chance to marry before the helicopter accident took her life. "Unless it's important to you. You've never—"

"I have no big desire to do the storybook wedding ceremony, if that's what's concerning you. I promise I don't care about any of that. I simply want you." He paused. "The sooner, the better."

In the distance, the skyline was speckled with brilliant lights. The busy sounds of the city served as a backdrop to her pounding heart. "How soon were you thinking? I mean, it's not been all that long since Shane had a wedding called off. I'm a bit worried that pushing ours on him this early will create unnecessary hurt. Aimee running out on him is still pretty fresh, you know? My little brother acts tough, but I know he's barely holding it together."

"Understandable," Evan said, agreeing. "Look, I think I have a solution." A slow grin formed on his face. He turned to face her, took her shoulders in his hands. "Let's elope."

"Elope? I thought you said your surprises were over."

"Think about it, Christel. We could cancel our charter flight and get a hotel. Tomorrow morning, we'll go to the courthouse and get our license. Then, we'll arrange for a judge and hold the ceremony right then and there. Just you and me."

Christel felt blood rush to her face. "Tomorrow? You want to do this tomorrow? What about a dress? I don't have a dress."

He laughed. "Yes, tomorrow. And there are stores in Honolulu. I'm sure they sell dresses." A smile nipped at the corners of his mouth. "So, babe. What do you say? We don't need all the pomp and circumstance. We only need each other."

Christel quickly ran through all the consequences of making such a rash decision in her mind. Her mother might be hurt, if excluded. Of course, her mother would also agree that a wedding might push Shane into having to face, yet again, what he'd recently lost. In that regard, it would be more kind to simply announce they'd been wed.

Katie would throw a fit but Christel knew her sister would often cool off as quickly as she heated up over something. Aiden would simply be happy for them. So would Uncle Jack and her mother's sister, Aunt Vanessa. Besides, her mother could still hold a reception party at her house, maybe outside by the pool.

Christel weighed all these thoughts briefly. Before she could change her mind, she nodded. "Let's do it!"

3

Sun spilled through the hotel window, bringing with it a new morning. Christel opened her eyes to find an empty space beside her. She sat up and glanced around the suite.

"Babe? What are you doing?" she asked as she spotted Evan in the other room, in a robe and sitting in a chair with his back to her. He turned and raised a finger. At that point, she could see he held his phone to his ear.

She climbed from the bed and wrapped her hotel robe around her, then wandered barefoot into the kitchenette hoping to find a coffee pot. As she neared, the aroma of freshly brewed coffee told her Evan had been considerate and made her some already.

He rarely drank coffee, claiming he felt better if he stuck to hot lemon water. "It has many health benefits," he had explained to her, early in their relationship. "Hot lemon water aids digestion and helps avoid kidney stones. Coffee dehydrates your system and raises your blood pressure slightly, while hot lemon water hydrates your system, which is good for your skin," he'd told her.

She looked at him with impatience. "Okay, okay, Dr. Matisse. So noted." she replied while refilling her cup...for the third time. It was a standing joke between them that her coffee addiction was not up for discussion.

Christel smiled at the past memory. Even more, when she recalled what had transpired the night before. She poured her coffee, admiring the diamond on her hand. It was true what she'd heard in television commercials. Diamonds really could look like fire and ice, all at once. She'd even give in to the notion diamonds could be a girl's best friend—especially when the luxurious stone represented a bright and happy future with someone you adored.

"Okay, yeah. Ultrasound is better than arthography in determining the stability of minimally placed lateral humeral condyle fractures in children." He saw her watching him and smiled. He silently mouthed, "I won't be long."

She smiled back at him and carried her steaming mug out to the balcony that overlooked the city. The streets below were already bustling at this time of the morning. Delivery truck drivers honked their horns at lines of cars ahead of them. Harried-looking workers with newspapers rolled under their arms and carrying Styrofoam cups scrambled down the sidewalk. A flower shop owner unfurled an awning over her shop window, then pulled out several buckets filled with blooms, positioning them by the open doorway. She looked up, spotted Christel on the balcony, and waved. Christel returned the greeting by wiggling her fingers in the air.

Suddenly, she felt Evan's arms around her waist. She leaned back into his strong chest and he kissed the back of her neck.

"Are you ready for the big day?" he whispered into her ear.

She turned in his arms and nodded. "Admittedly, I barely slept last night. So much was swirling in my head. You sure know how to knock a girl off her feet."

"You haven't changed your mind, have you?" he teased.

"Absolutely not," she declared. As if to place an exclamation mark at the end of her verbal sentence, she reached and kissed him.

He picked up on the cue and pulled her tighter against him. His lips pressed against her own, long and hard and wanting. There were a lot of things she had missed as a divorced woman. She'd missed a man's physical touch, his need for her. This was high on the list.

After several long seconds, Evan finally pulled back. He playfully popped her on the behind. "Better get moving, my soon-to-be bride. We have a lot to do before I make you my wife forever."

She found the perfect dress at a boutique located only a few blocks from the hotel. From the moment she tried on the knee-length, white-satin sheath with an overlay of lace and a drop-shoulder collar that would rival something you might see on Audrey Hepburn, she was sold. It was classic, simple, and elegant.

The helpful clerk brought out the perfect matching satin heels with pretty white bows. "Do you like these?"

"Oh, goodness. Yes." Christel smiled back at the young girl. "I love them."

Christel had the clerk package up the purchases and directed that they be delivered to their hotel room, where Christel would get ready. Evan would wear the suit he had on the night before.

Hand in hand, they wandered over to the flower shop Christel had spotted. The owner immediately recognized her. "What can I help you with this morning?"

Christel explained they were going to be married. She needed something to carry, nothing too flashy or large. She preferred a tiny spray of fragrant blooms. And not lilies of the valley.

The lady went into coolers in the back room and appeared

holding a dainty bouquet made with a single shell-pink gerbera daisy, two light pink rose buds, two small white anemones, surrounded with sprigs of dusty sage foliage and delicate white gypsophila. Again, the selection was just what she'd hoped for. Simple, but elegant.

After securing their marriage license, she and Evan returned to the hotel where they enjoyed room service. Christel could barely eat for her nerves. Was she doing the right thing? Eloping?

One look at the handsome man sitting across the table reminded her she absolutely had no wish to change her mind. Within hours she was going to be Mrs. Evan Matisse.

The name rolled around in her mind, foreign and comforting, all at the same time.

When they'd finished eating their salads, Evan stood and held out his hand. "You ready?" he asked.

Christel confidently placed her hand in his.

Yes...she was ready.

Evan had arranged for the ceremony to take place on a grass-covered outcropping overlooking the ocean. A judge would officiate.

Christel found her heart pounding as she stepped into place. The weather was perfect, sunny and warm, but not hot. A slight ocean breeze caught the tendrils hanging from her updo and in the distance, waves crashed against rock.

She held her bouquet. Evan wore a lei made of white plumeria blooms. They both wore wide smiles as the officiant cleared his throat. "Dearly, beloved. We are gathered here today to celebrate one of life's greatest moments. The joining of two hearts, two lives, two futures."

Evan looked at her with tears sprouting in his eyes. He quickly wiped the moisture away and directed his attention back to the judge.

"The Hawaiian word for love is aloha—sacrificial love.

Unbroken bond of commitment to each other. No greater blessing of happiness can come to you than to keep this understanding of your marriage alive in the days ahead. May your aloha continuously grow more true and more wonderful with each day."

He reached behind him to the linen-draped table that had been set up. On it, were three glass containers. The two smaller ones were filled with sand. The judge passed the sand-filled containers to Christel and Evan. Then, he held up the third—a large, intricately carved vase. "Evan and Christel, you are about to seal your relationship by pledging to commit to one another through your lives. This is symbolized through the pouring of these two containers of sand. One, representing you, Evan. The other representing you, Christel—and all that you both were, all that you are, and all that you will ever be."

He smiled and instructed them to blend the sand by pouring the contents of their individual container into the large vase. "As you both pour your sand into the third container, the sand in the individual containers will no longer exist, but will be joined as one. Just as these grains of sand can never be separated, my prayer for you today is that your lives together would be blended likewise and never dissipate in the changing tides of life."

He looked to Evan. "Evan, please take your bride's hand and repeat after me. Do you, Evan, take Christel to be your lawfully wedded wife, to love, honor, and cherish her all the days of your life?"

Evan sniffed and choked out a simple reply. "Yes, I do."

The judge turned to Christel. "Do you, Christel, take Evan to be your lawfully wedded husband, to love, honor, and support him all the days of your life?"

She nodded. "I do."

A large smile broke across the judge's face. "Then, in the

power awarded me by the state of Hawaii, I now pronounce you husband, and wife."

Evan leaned, took her face in his hands and kissed her.

At that moment, Jon's uninvited image appeared in her mind. A strange sadness mixed with her joy.

Christel immediately pushed the unwelcome feeling aside, and kissed Evan back. She had a new life now, one filled with love and faithfulness. As they parted, she laughed and threw her bouquet into the sea, feeling immense elation.

She was now Mrs. Evan Matisse.

4

Ava finished examining the inventories and closed out the file on her laptop. Before she could open the cashflow projections Christel had prepared, there was a light knock. She looked up to see her sister, Vanessa, smiling back at her from the doorway.

"Hey, long time no see."

Ava sighed and closed her laptop. "What do you mean? We saw each other yesterday."

"In passing." Vanessa pointed to the empty guest chair in front of Ava's desk. "Do you mind?"

Ava looked across the desk warily as her sister sat. "Is there something up?"

Rarely did her sister just pop in unless she wanted something. While Ava and Vanessa had called a truce on their years long splintering, they still weren't exactly chummy. They'd spend time together, but normally in a group setting. Ava wished it were different, but she'd acquiesced to the fact some relationships were simply not that close.

"I need your advice."

Ava's brows lifted. She placed crossed arms on the desk with interest. "My advice?"

"Yes. As you know, the only job I've ever really known was in television. I worked terribly hard to get that lead anchor chair, only to be let go." Her sister paused and picked a loose string off her linen slacks. "It's been over half a year, and I'm worried about my finances. I am so grateful you extended the offer for me to stay in one of the worker shanties. Frankly, that saved my bacon."

Ava gave her sister a weak smile, wishing she'd get to the point. She still had a lot to accomplish today. Sitting here chatting was not getting any of those tasks done.

"I know you're tight for time, so let me get to the point. I've been offered a job."

"A job? I thought you already had a job."

Her sister shrugged. "I'm currently working a temporary job. I never expected to be a hotel concierge forever. Plus, the hours..." She waved off the idea. "Well, working nights and weekends is getting very old. It's hard to juggle a social life when you work at the very time most people are out enjoying themselves."

"You've been dating—a lot," Ava pointed out. "I see men over at your place at least twice a week." *And rarely the same guy*, she thought.

Vanessa gave Ava a look that warned her not to start. As if remembering she needed Ava, her scowl morphed into a pasted smile. "Like I said, I need your advice. I've been offered a job. I think I'd like to take it."

Ava leaned back in her chair and steepled her fingers. "But?"

Vanessa drew a deep breath. "Well, my boss would be one of the guys I've dated."

"Oh, yeah. Not a good idea."

Vanessa leaned forward. "But it's an amazing job, Ava. I'd be working with Jim Kahele."

"The councilman running for state senator? You dated Jim Kahele?"

Her sister rolled her eyes. "We went out to dinner a few times. I really like him but he isn't my type. He works far too many hours, and...well, he's not a lot of fun. But he is a really smart guy," she rushed to add. "He's well-connected and he thinks I'd be a great addition to the campaign team."

"Doing what?" Her sister was a lot of things, but she'd never been especially interested in politics, and she mentioned exactly that. "This seems a little out of your wheelhouse."

"It's exactly in line with my skill set. Jim wants me to be the Communications Director and Media Liaison. Given my background in television, I would be perfect for the job. Think of all those interviews I've done over the years at election time."

"But you were fired for slipping up on a matter related to politics."

"Not exactly politics," Vanessa argued. "I simply made a statement that station management believed contradicted the viewpoint of most of our Seattle audience. They worried when the ratings plummeted. If they hadn't been so quick to throw me under the bus the ratings would have corrected. There were plenty of viewers who believed like I did. I have the emails to prove it."

"Be that as it may, are you sure you want to work in such a volatile environment?"

Vanessa revealed what the position paid.

"Oh." It's all Ava could think to say. From a financial standpoint, she could see why her sister would entertain the offer.

"So, what do you think? Should I take it?"

Ava shook her head. "That's a hard one. I mean, you'd be reporting to someone you had a relationship with and all. That can get really sticky. Are you sure of his motives?"

"Dinner out a couple of times hardly counts as a relationship. And his only motive is to put together the best team he can."

"Well, still..." Ava let her thought drift off. They both knew Vanessa had already made up her mind. She simply wanted Ava to put a seal of approval on her decision.

This was her sister's modus operandi. She rarely conformed to what people expected but wanted pats on the back anyway.

Her sister always did exactly what she wanted to do, regardless of consequences, or wise counsel. How many times had Vanessa been warned that her daughter would grow up resentful of her mother putting her career before her ball games, her school plays, even holiday dinners. Vanessa's choices had ultimately cost her a marriage and her family. Now, her daughter refused to even visit, let alone live with her according to the shared custody agreement.

Ava simply looked over at her sister. "So, what are you going to do?"

"These opportunities don't present often. And I don't need to remind you how thin my budget has been." Vanessa straightened in the chair. "I'm going to take it." She stood and pulled her buzzing phone from her purse.

"Was there ever a doubt?" Ava muttered under her breath.

"I'm sorry. What?" Vanessa glanced at her phone and incoming text message. "Well, look. I know you're busy." She wandered around the desk and pulled Ava into a light hug. "Thanks for your input. I really appreciate it, Sis."

Ava gave her a weak smile. "Glad I could help."

She watched Vanessa leave and close the door behind her, then leaned back in her chair, remembering when she and Vanessa were little girls. Ava loved to play Monopoly. Vanessa could barely get to the point where she had enough money to buy a house before she ditched and quit playing.

"Let's play the Dating Game instead," her sister suggested. Vanessa loved to open the little white door to find out if her date matched the outfit cards in her hand. "Careful, Ava. You don't want to get the dud!"

Even back then, they'd rarely seen the world the same.

5

Katie tapped her fingers impatiently against the counter as she waited for the Keurig to finish dripping. When her mug was finally full, she carried her coffee out to the new wraparound deck. Building this house had been both exhilarating and grueling. While she loved working with the famous architect, Jasmit Tan, her overzealous dedication to the project and her spending had rattled her marriage. Standing out on the deck with her coffee in hand, she admired the magnificent view of the Pacific Ocean, a panoramic vista that made the ordeal worth it.

"Mom!" Willa called from inside. "Your phone is buzzing."

Katie reluctantly pulled her attention from the distant ocean and headed back inside. She picked up her phone from the counter and brought it to her ear. "Shane? Why are you calling so early? It's not even seven."

"Don't talk to me about early," her brother groaned. "The baby had me up all night. I overslept because I kept hitting snooze on my alarm. Now, I'm running late for work. And what do I find? A dead battery."

"And you called me why?"

"I need you to come get me and Carson, drop him off at daycare and take me to the boat landing. Hopefully, Uncle Jack will hold the tour for me."

Katie sighed and weighed her answer. She wanted to argue she had a long list of things to do. Frankly, her schedule since completing the house was fairly light. She could run the gift shop and the tours in her sleep. "So, little brother. What's in it for me?"

"I'll love you forever?"

That made Katie laugh. "You already do."

She hung up and dumped her now cold coffee into the sink.

Willa crammed her math book inside her backpack. "You know, if I had my driver's license, I could play chauffeur to Uncle Shane. And I could do the grocery shopping. And—"

Katie held up her hands. "Okay, okay. Message received. Same message I received yesterday and the day before."

"Well, I'm just saying." Her daughter scooped up her backpack and slung it over her shoulder. She gave Katie a peck on the cheek before heading out to meet the school bus.

"See you tonight," Katie called after her.

Katie grabbed her set of keys and slipped the strap of her purse over her shoulder. She bent to pick up Noelle. "Do Mommy a favor, sweetheart. Stay little. We can't afford teenagers on our car insurance."

Noelle's eyes lit up. "Zoom, zoom!"

As Katie headed out the door, she nearly ran into her mother who stood ready to ring the doorbell. "Mom? What are you doing here?"

"Have you heard from Christel? She hasn't shown up to work and we have a meeting in a little over an hour from now with that new golf course architect, the one who used to work with Rees Jones." She lifted her wrist and checked her Apple watch. "It's not like her to be late."

Katie pulled the door closed and locked it. "Did you try calling her?"

Her mother nodded. "Several times."

"Well, she had a big date with Evan last night, I do know that. Maybe they had a long night and she simply overslept and isn't answering her phone messages." She gave her mom a wink. "Or, maybe he's still there."

Ava waved off the suggestion. "More than a mother needs to know."

An idea spawned. "Look, I have to go get Shane and Carson. But, if you want, I can rush back. I'll attend the meeting with you."

Her mother looked reluctant. "Oh, I don't know. Christel has all the financials. Maybe I should postpone until this afternoon."

"She sent me the P&L projections too. While I won't be able to provide input on the budgets, I can take careful notes until Christel shows up. That will free you to focus on your exchange with the designer." *Besides*, Katie thought, *I could use the mental stimulation*. She might not be an attorney or accountant, but she was fully capable of providing valuable input on this kind of project. Hadn't she just built a house that was enviable in architectural circles? She could do this.

She stared at her mom, waiting.

"I guess it couldn't hurt," her mother conceded. "If you think you can get back before he arrives."

Katie's face broke into a bright grin. "I will absolutely be back in time." She kissed her mother's cheek and rushed for her car.

Perhaps it was time to reconsider and let Willa get her driver's license. Might come in handy for times just like today.

∼

CHRISTEL DRUMMED her fingers on the armrest. "How long before we land?" she asked Evan for the fourth time.

"Honey, we can't make the plane go any faster."

Christel groaned and leaned her head against the seatback. "I can't believe I forgot about that meeting." She grabbed her phone and tried to send her text again only to get another error message.

Evan reached over and lightly rubbed the back of her neck. "No cell service in the air," he reminded.

Christel knew that. She simply wasn't thinking. Her nerves were off the charts. She hadn't felt like this since oversleeping on the morning of an important exam in college. She hated that feeling in her gut, the one that reminded her she was dropping a ball and letting someone down with little control to change it.

"Do I need to remind you, Mrs. Matisse, that we are still officially on our honeymoon?" Evan's eyes twinkled as he took her hand and squeezed it.

Christel stifled a moan. "I should never have agreed to stay over another night." She looked over at her new husband. "Guess I just got swept away. My good-looking husband has that effect on me," she teased.

There was little she could do about missing that meeting. She needed to let it go.

Even so, she lifted her wrist and checked her watch again.

6

Ava quickly looked over the package Christel had prepared which included a curriculum vitae for the guy she was meeting with this morning. His name was Tom Strobe and he had graduated from Texas A&M with honors. After working abroad for two years, he joined Rees Jones, Inc. He was a member of the American Society of Golf Course Architects and served as president for two consecutive years. He had recently left and started his own firm, taking with him a long list of notable projects he'd worked on over the years.

Impressive.

Ava gathered the development package and headed for her office door. She stepped into the warm morning air and noticed a blue SUV making its way up the long drive. "That must be him now," she muttered and checked her watch. "Right on time."

The car came to a stop and a man climbed out. He waved in her direction.

She headed that way. "You must be Mr. Strobe." She extended a hand.

"Tom," he corrected. "I still consider Mr. Strobe to be my father." The corners of his mouth lifted in a warm smile and he took her hand and shook. "It's really nice to finally meet. Your daughter has told me all about you and this operation. I'm looking forward to partnering with Pali Maui on this project."

Ava apologized for Christel's absence. "I'm sure she'll be here at any moment." Her phone buzzed signaling an incoming text. She lifted her phone. The message was from Christel.

"I'm SO sorry, Mom. At the airport. Just landed and waiting for clearance to taxi in to the terminal which is taking forever. I'll be there as soon as I can and will fill you in on details."

Ava pocketed the phone. "That was Christel. Apparently, she's been held up at the airport and will be here as soon as she can."

Tom shot her a relaxed smile. "No worries. I've blocked out the entire day."

"Let's take a look at our current golf course while we wait for her." Ava invited him to follow her.

She guessed him to be only slightly younger than Lincoln. He was tall, had short cropped brown hair, and wore jeans and a button-down in a nice shade of blue, one that matched his eyes. She also noticed he wore the same cologne she'd bought for Lincoln the last Christmas they spent together.

"So, you recently relocated to the island?" she asked, attempting to make small talk.

Tom nodded. "It's always been a dream of mine. After years spent living in big cities, I yearned for an escape to warmer climates and a more laidback lifestyle." His eyes twinkled, magnifying the crinkle lines at his eyes. "The ocean and palm trees didn't hurt."

"Yes, Maui attracts a lot of tourists and many of them plan to retire here. That is, until they discover how expensive it is."

He nodded. "It is that. Fortunately, my father left me a house and some property that had been passed to him by my grandfather, who was stationed at Pearl Harbor in 1943. You'd have thought the attack would hold bad memories, but he fell in love with the islands...and with my grandmother who was native Hawaiian." He laughed.

Ava couldn't contain her smile. "Well, yes. Love dictates a lot of decisions." She glanced at the hand carrying his clipboard. No ring.

They passed the guest parking lot outside the famed restaurant where her son-in-law was master chef. Even at this early hour, food aromas wafted in the air.

Tom motioned. "I hear No Ka 'Oi has superb food. I've been wanting to try it but reservations are booked weeks in advance. I can't seem to get my act together and get on the list. I travel a lot of the time, often without much notice," he explained. "Because of that, I barely know what I'm doing that far out."

She grinned. "Well, I happen to know someone who could move you to the top of the list. Please, just call me. Anytime."

He thanked her as they stepped onto the winding foot path leading to the golf course. "Pali Maui is as impressive as what I'd read and heard about." He complimented their reputation as one of the most respected pineapple operations on the islands, or anywhere else, for that matter.

She explained a bit of the history. "It seems we have some things in common. My father was a Pearl Harbor buff. He moved us here after my mother died of cancer. He bought a faltering pineapple operation on island as a write-off—an operation that eventually became Pali Maui. I inherited it after he died of a stroke ten years ago. I always intended to turn it into a family-run business. I'm partially successful with that notion. My oldest daughter, Christel, is our chief financial officer and also oversees legal aspects. My younger daughter, Katie, manages the gift shop and tours. Her husband is our chef at No Ka 'Oi. Both of my boys are involved in other pursuits, for the time being. Eventually, I hope to capture them as well."

They both laughed.

"I envy you having a family."

She spotted a touch of sadness in his voice. "You don't?"

Tom shook his head. "Early in my career, I was married solely to my job. Ten years ago, I took the plunge and finally said I do. Two years later, she said I don't."

"Oh, I'm so sorry."

He smiled back at her. "Don't be. I've had a good life."

Before he could say more, Katie rushed up behind them. "Sorry, I'm late. I hurried to get back but traffic was a bear. Some accident or something. Nothing serious, but it held up cars for over a half hour." Breathless, she extended her hand to Tom. "I'm Katie."

Ava made introductions. "This is the daughter I told you about. She runs the gift shop and tours. She's very talented," she added, unsure why she felt the need to build up her daughter. Perhaps it was because Katie always seemed adrift, like she had yet to find her purpose.

As they approached the clubhouse, Ava turned to Tom. "I'm afraid your job is cut out for you. We've been thinking of renovating for years. We had to wait for the right time financially."

Tom surveyed the vista filled with sprawling fairways. "I beg to differ. The existing course is already enviable. Still, I think we can transform it into something spectacular, a destination course that could place you in the sight of the PGA for tournaments."

Katie pointed. "Here comes Christel."

Ava and Tom turned their attention to where she pointed. Christel waved in their direction. As she approached, Ava took the opportunity to praise her other daughter. "Christel has been a huge asset to Pali Maui. Not only is she a certified public accountant and a master at tracking cash flow, financial planning and analyzing the company's financial strengths and weaknesses, she also has a law degree. She's been invaluable in developing and proposing strategic directions for our company."

"I apologize for my tardy arrival," Christel said as she met up with them. She extended her hand. "So nice to finally meet you, Tom."

Katie leaned closer. "Is that a wedding ring?" she blurted.

Christel instinctively pulled her hand back.

"That's a wedding ring," Katie exclaimed. She flipped around to Ava. "Mom, Christel is wearing a wedding ring."

Christel let out a sigh. "Okay, okay...not to take over this important meeting..." She gave an apologetic smile in Tom's direction. "But, yes. Evan and I were married last night."

Ava's hand went to her chest. "What? You were married?"

Katie parked her hands on her hips. "Without telling us first? Without inviting us?"

Christel's face flushed as she quickly glanced over at Tom, then back at Katie. "Can we please discuss this later?"

Katie would have none of it. "But, we're your family. You left us out of one of the most important days of your entire life. You got married without us."

"I said, we'll deal with this at another time." She didn't hide her annoyance with her sister. "When we can talk privately."

Ava leaned over close to Tom and whispered, "So, are you still wanting that family?"

7

Mig Nakamoa walked into the south packing shed. "Hey, Fred!" he called out as he headed in the direction of the shift manager. "According to yesterday's inventory manifests, the pineapples aren't making it into storage fast enough. We don't want to risk Thielaviopsis rot setting in." To further make his point, he lifted the pineapple he was carrying. "The stem of the crown on this is darkening. With the high temps we're experiencing on the island this week, the fruit could develop further black rot."

"Sorry, Mig. We had a short crew yesterday. But, we'll do better."

Mig patted Fred firmly on the shoulder. "Thanks. That's why I brought it to your attention. I knew I could count on you to remedy the situation." He gave his trusted shift manager a nod. "We still on for our backgammon game tonight?"

"Wouldn't miss it. Under the pergola?"

Mig nodded. "Yup. And bring your best game. As you know, there's money riding on this one."

Fred's face broke into a wide grin. "Money that's going home in my pocket."

Mig laughed before he turned and headed back outside where he climbed on his UTV, a gift from Ava only months before.

Mig knew he was fortunate to be working for the Briscoe family. Not only were they generous, but he appreciated partnering with Ava's effort to be the best in the industry. That woman cut no corners when it came to pineapple production.

Over the years, the Briscoes had become his *ohana pili pili*. This family had embraced him and made him feel important... both professionally, and personally.

He'd watched those kids grow up. They were like his own.

Mig started up is UTV and headed for the heavily scented pineapple fields where he would spend the next hours inspecting the parameters. There could be no breaches or holes in the fencing or wild feral pigs would get in.

Feral swine generally traveled in family groups, called sounders, composed of two or more adult sows and their young. Sounders can vary in size, including a few individuals to as many as thirty. A group that size could easily destroy an area the size of a football field in a matter of hours.

When Mig finished hours later, he returned to the packing sheds to find Wimberly Ann's empty car parked. The sight made him smile.

It'd only been hours since he'd bid her goodbye after she spent the night with him for the first time, a night filled with passion he'd long since forgotten how to feel. Something about Wimberly Ann made him young again. Everything was better with her around. Smells were sharper. Colors more vibrant. The donuts he adored were sweeter.

"Yoo-hoo...there you are!" she called out when she spotted him from the open packing shed door. She held up a plate wrapped with aluminum foil. "I baked you some chocolate chip macadamia nut cookies, my specialty."

He quickly moved to join her. As he bent to brush a kiss

against her cheek, he noticed she smelled like pachouli and maple syrup. "You smell good," he whispered against her ear.

She batted her long lashes. "Why thank you, Mr. Nakamoa." She held up the plate. "The cookies are still warm."

He gratefully extracted the plate from her hand and pulled back the foil. "Mmm...they look good." He hoisted a large one from the center of the plate and took a big bite. Still chewing, he told her, "They are every bit as good as you smell."

The sound of a baby crying diverted their attention in the direction of the worker shanties in the distance. "Looks like Shane is over visiting his Aunt Vanessa." Mig glanced at his watch. "He must've finished up work early today."

Wimberly Ann made a tsking sound and shook her head. "That poor boy. To be left at the altar like that. Heartbreaking."

Mig agreed. "Things can go along fine and dandy and then someone rips your heart out and stomps on it. Happens all the time."

Wimberly Ann nested her head against Mig's chest. "Not in all situations, baby. Especially not with me."

AVA WALKED Tom to his car. "Thank you, Tom. And I'm sorry about the girls. Sometimes they still act like the same teenagers who squabbled over which of the Backstreet Boys was better looking...Nick Carter or Howie Dorough. Still, it's rare for either of them to argue like that now, especially in public."

Tom laughed.

"Of course, the fact that Christel eloped last night did come as a surprise. My girls are close and learning her sister snuck off and got married knocked Katie for a loop."

"I can imagine." He seemed to slow his pace. "And what about you? Did the news knock you for a loop?"

Normally, a question of that sort might be considered inappropriate in a business setting. Yet, Tom was the sort of person who made you feel entirely comfortable. They had a lot in common. Ava could see them becoming friends.

"Actually, I'm happy for Christel," she told him. Ava shared her oldest daughter's history, leaving out anything she deemed inappropriate to tell a stranger, especially a business associate. "Evan Matisse is a really nice man. I only hope she is happy."

Inside, Ava knew that to be true. She also wanted her daughter to feel safe and secure again. Journeying through Jay's addiction had been grueling. So had the decision to finally leave him after realizing there was little chance of remedying the situation. Until Jay wanted to be sober, there wasn't much Christel could do except go down with him. Ava would always be glad her daughter had found the strength to move on and start over. Yes, it had been hard. Christel had loved Jay intensely, but love didn't fix everything. That was a lesson she and her daughter had both learned.

When the family had all first met Evan as Aiden's doctor after the accident, Ava carried a tiny whisper of hope that the spark she'd noticed between Evan and Christel would turn into something more.

They reached Tom's SUV. He slapped the back of his clipboard with his hand. "Well, this initial meeting has been very productive. After seeing the layout of the current fairways and greens, I now have a better sense of where we are heading."

"Yes," Ava agreed. "I think this was a great first step."

Their eyes met. The way Tom gazed at her caught her a little off guard. She quickly looked away. "So, until next time?"

He smiled back at her. "Until next time."

8

Christel opened the door to her mother's house and was immediately met with falling confetti and shouts of congratulations. She turned to Evan with a grin. "See? I told you my family would never let our marriage pass without a big celebration."

He burst into laughter and brushed some confetti from his thick black hair. "So noted."

Aiden placed his hand on Evan's shoulder. "Do I still call you doctor now that you're my brother-in-law?"

Evan smiled. "I've not been Dr. Matisse to this family for a while now, and that's more than fine by me."

Katie took hold of Christel's hand and pulled her further inside the room. "I'm still pouting over missing the actual ceremony, but we're here to celebrate the big event now. I hope you know how happy Jon and I are for you. You deserve every bit of happiness."

Willa nodded from her spot on the sofa. "Impressive. It's pretty difficult to keep anything from this family. Especially something this big."

Shane lifted tiny Carson in the air and wiggled him. Looks

of delight formed on his little son's face. "Yeah, Sis. Good move." He looked at his new brother-in-law. "I'd shake, but my hands are a bit full at the moment. I will buy you a beer, though." He hollered over at Katie. "Get Evan a beer, would you?"

"What did you wear?" Wimberly Ann gushed. "I hope you took lots of photos."

"We did arrange for a photographer to take a few. Here, let me show you." Christel pulled out her phone and handed it over to Wimberly Ann.

"Oh my goodness! That dress!" She turned to face Mig. "Sugar, will you look at that dress! Have you seen anything so stunning?"

Katie stood on her tippy toes and leaned over Wimberly Ann's shoulder. "Let me see." She scrutinized the image, then maneuvered her position and lifted the phone from Wimberly Ann's hand. She scrolled through, peering at each of the photographs. "Is this all?" she asked. "There's only four."

Christel laughed. "How many photographs of the happy couple standing on a cliff with the ocean in the backdrop does one need?"

Katie huffed. "But where's the one of the kiss? Where's the one of you saying your vows?"

Ava gently lifted the phone from her younger daughter's hand. "Let me see." She browsed the photos with Alani next to her.

"Oh, honey. These are so beautiful," her mom said.

"Yes, you look so happy." Alani planted a kiss on both of Christel's cheeks. "Both Elta and I pray you have many joyful years ahead."

Christel expressed her concern over hurting their feelings. In the past, every Briscoe wedding had been held at Wailea Seaside Chapel with Elta officiating.

Alani's husband waved off her uneasiness. "What matters is

that God was there. Like Alani, I pray He greatly blesses the covenant you made to one another."

"Thank you. That means so much to me." Christel leaned and gave their family friend a hug. Over his shoulder, she spotted their son, Ori. Her friend winked and silently mouthed his congratulations.

Alani picked up a large platter mounded with cold shrimp. "Where are you going on your honeymoon?"

Christel glanced at her new husband. "Oh, that's going to have to wait. This entire wedding thing was rather sudden and unplanned. Both Evan and I have heavy schedules with commitments that aren't easily moved."

"Aye, young people have priorities all mixed up. Take the honeymoon. There will be years ahead of you to work." She carried the platter into the living area and placed it on the coffee table.

"Tell that to the people needing surgery, right Evan?" She bent and grabbed a shrimp. "We'll plan something fabulous, as soon as the golf course renovation is underway. We're at the beginning of the project, the stage where everything teeters in the tenuous zone, especially the financial aspect. We secured construction loan approval, but the commitment doesn't cover the entire cost of renovation. Luckily, one of the bank's board members recommended an investor willing to extend the necessary short-term capital via a bridge loan secured with the profits from our fall crop."

Ori helped himself to a shrimp. "I knew you hoped to renovate the golf course at some point in the future but didn't realize you'd moved forward. Glad to hear it. I love to golf."

From his position on the sofa, Aiden leaned his elbows on his knees. "Sounds risky."

Christel shrugged. "Every expansion of this sort has risk. You simply weigh how much you're willing to take on. It's the reason we've waited until now. It's finally the right time."

Ava carried a bowl filled with olives and placed them on a side table. "We just went under contract with Tom Strobe, a golf architect who has worked with Rees Jones on some of the most outstanding courses on the PGA tournament circuit. He believes this renovation could put us in those circles. Just imagine how much free publicity that will bring to our brand."

Katie parked her hands on her hips. "Excuse me. This is a wedding celebration. Let's end the business talk, shall we?"

Willa nodded her agreement. "Yeah, all that financial talk is boring. Let's hurry and get to the part where Aunt Christel and Uncle Evan cut the cake." She paused and looked over at him. "Gee, that sounds so strange. Uncle Evan," she repeated.

Evan clasped his hands and rubbed them together. "And a grand cake it is." He knelt and looked into little Noelle's eyes. "I love cake, don't you?"

She giggled and nodded with enthusiasm. "Cake! Cake!"

Willa examined the wedding cake, a white three-tiered masterpiece decorated with confectionery pearls and real crème-colored plumeria blooms. "It is amazing."

Katie patted her daughter on the back. "Do you remember telling us you wanted a Sponge Bob wedding cake?" She popped an olive in her mouth and began chewing.

Willa rolled her eyes. "I was six, Mom."

"I know we've moved off the subject," Aiden said. "But I'm curious. Who is the investor making the bridge loan?"

Christel leaned her head against her new husband's shoulder. "It's a company, actually. Latham Enterprises headquartered in Honolulu."

Katie choked and coughed up little pieces of olive. "Latham Enterprises?" she managed between coughs and fighting for air.

Ava repeatedly slapped her daughter's back, just like when she was little and choked on a piece of food. "Honey, are you okay?"

Katie managed to nod, but she suddenly looked anything but okay.

∽

KATIE FELT RINGING in her ears. Did her sister say that Pali Maui was obtaining financial assistance from Latham Enterprises? Surely she had heard wrong.

Latham was the same outfit Katie met with and failed to secure a deal for the manufacturing idea she had. Greer Latham was the guy who...she fought to catch her breath.

"Katie? What's the matter?" Aiden asked, concerned.

Evan immediately came alongside her, put his arms around her shoulders, and led her to the sofa. "Sit. We don't want you to have a syncope episode."

"Syncope?" Shane asked.

Christel nodded. "Medical term for fainting."

Shane shrugged. "Oh, why didn't he just say that?"

Ava knelt in front of her daughter. "Honey, I agree with Evan. You look like you're going to pass out."

"Maybe she's pregnant," Willa blurted. "Would be my luck. One more sibling to have to babysit." The comment earned her a few pointed stares. "What?" she asked. "You try juggling homework with crying little sisters."

Katie heard them all talking, but her mind wouldn't engage. All she could think about was Greer Latham. Not long after her father died, Katie took a trip to Honolulu hoping to convince an investor to invest in her plan to expand the gift shop. That investor was Greer Latham.

Unfortunately, he offered her a ride to the airport. On the way, he made an inappropriate pass. There was no mistaking his intention. He would extend the loan with the expectation that she pay it back...with interest. Costly interest that she was unwilling to pay.

As soon as the car drew to a stop at a red light, she bolted from the car.

The worst thing is that she had never told anyone about the incident, not even Jon. Her hopes to measure up with Christel and strengthen the family business had gone down in flames. She was horribly ashamed that she had been so gullible. The ill-fated incident forced her to question whether she'd been wrong and was not cut out to be a businesswoman like her sister, after all.

"Honey?" her mom repeated.

Alani thrust a glass of water into her hands. "Drink, honey."

Katie did as she was told. She drank slowly, trying to collect herself and her thoughts.

No doubt, she was now in a horrible position. She had to tell Christel and her mom, didn't she? If she revealed what had happened, she'd look like an idiot. Jon would be mad she never told him.

Yet, Pali Maui was partnering with a creep. A scoundrel who could not be trusted.

Katie handed the glass back to Alani after nearly emptying it. "Thanks," she told her mom's best friend.

Yes, she had to reveal what she knew regardless of the consequences. There was simply too much at stake to keep what she'd learned about Greer Latham to herself. Obviously, now was not the time for bad news. She wouldn't steal Christel's joyous moment.

She was going to have to tell them.

Not yet...but very soon.

9

One look at the steep staircase and Vanessa knew this just wasn't going to work in heels. She craned her neck in all directions to make sure no one was watching, then she slipped off her pumps and took the stairs barefoot, two at a time.

She'd barely been able to sleep the night before, anticipating her first day at the campaign headquarters.

Communications Director and Media Liaison.

Vanessa couldn't help but smile. The title had a nice ring to it.

She stopped at the top of the stairs, her legs burning, and slipped her heels back in place, then glanced around until she located the right door. She smoothed her carefully chosen red skirt and headed that way. Red was a known power color.

The campaign offices were located on the top floor of the Marketplace in Lahaina. A smart move, given the foot traffic and visibility. It never hurt to have passersby have a visual reminder that Jim Kahele was vying to be their representative in the US Senate.

If Jim won the primary, they'd also need to open an office in Honolulu.

Her mind was already spinning with a slew of ideas. One of her first tasks would be to remodel the window signage. It needed to be eye-catching and pop with patriotism. On top of her task list was to develop a strong brand with a logo that reflected their message. Something subtle, but with the promise that sending Jim to Washington, DC would solve all their problems and concerns.

Before her hand could turn the knob, the door swung open.

"Vanessa!" Jim Kahele beckoned her inside. He gave her a quick hug. "We're so happy to have you on board."

"Thank you. I'm excited to be here."

He clasped his hands together and rubbed them in anticipation of what was to come. "First, let's introduce you to the team."

Vanessa had covered many political stories over the course of her media career. The campaign office was everything she had always encountered—small, yet functional. The walls were plastered with the obligatory campaign posters. Metal folding chairs lined several long tables stacked with campaign brochures along with envelopes waiting to be sealed. The smell of stale coffee drew her attention to a Keurig perched on a tiny wooden table that was littered with empty Styrofoam cups and used stirrers. An overflowing trash can provided a hint as to why.

Jim placed his hand at the small of her back and guided her to toward a cramped cubicle. Sitting inside, a woman with severe features and gray hair pulled tightly into a bun looked up as they approached. She wore no makeup, only a frown.

"This is my mother, Lucille," Jim said, making introductions.

Vanessa extended her hand thinking the two looked nothing alike. Jim's darker complexion was a stark contrast to his woman's face which was the color of uncooked chicken. She really needed some lipstick and a little blush. And a different hairstyle.

"Hello," Jim's mother muttered, reluctantly taking Vanessa's hand as if it were covered in motor oil. She felt something rub against her leg and looked down to find a large cat with fur the same color as Jim's mother's face. The animal wasn't just large, it could best be described as grossly overweight. The poor thing lumbered like it was carrying the weight of the world on its back. Maybe not on its back...but certainly there was a lot of weight around that cat's belly.

Jim saw her looking at the cat. "That's Axel, Mother's cat."

Vanessa didn't like cats. Especially in an office setting. Still, as a measure of goodwill, she leaned to pet its fur. She had barely grazed the cat's back when it turned and hissed. Before she could pull back, Axel clawed her, leaving a deep red gouge across the back of her right hand...a scratch that was already starting to bleed.

"Oh, my goodness! I'm so sorry," Jim apologized. He ran for the coffee station and grabbed some napkins and hurried back, placing them against her wound. "It is so unlike Axel to act like that."

Lucille nodded. "Yes, Axel normally warms to people he likes."

Vanessa tried to hide a scowl. The woman's implication was clear. Vanessa did not like cats, and apparently this cat did not like her.

Jim guided her to the next cubicle where a guy, who couldn't be a minute over twenty, sat. His necktie was loosened and his shirt sleeves were rolled. He had pencils tucked behind both ears and had his nose close to his computer screen. Seeing them approach, he pulled back from the article he'd been reading and stared in their direction.

"I'd like you to meet Scott BeVier. He's on loan to us from

the University of Nebraska as part of a political science intern program."

Scott stood and shook Vanessa's hand. "It's nice to meet you. Jim spoke highly of your skills."

Vanessa gave her benefactor a warm smile of gratitude. "I am delighted by this opportunity. Jim is a candidate I believe in. His policies are absolutely in line with what is good for this state. I'm happy to be a part of the team that will help him get elected." She widened her smile at her new boss. Based on the look on Jim's face, her volley back was well-received. She mentally shined her fingernails against her chest, pleased that all those years behind a camera charming viewers had not gone to waste.

There were three other staffers in the office, two middle-aged women and a balding man who looked to be in his sixties. All were full-time volunteers. Then there was the kid wearing a T-shirt who knelt plugging cords into what appeared to be a computer server. His name was Kickback, a nickname he'd earned as a surfer on the island waves commonly known as Jaws.

"I know he looks young," Jim confided as they moved on into his office. "But no one knows systems more than this kid."

Jim shut the door behind them. "So, what do you think?"

"I think your opponent doesn't stand a chance. Jim Kahele is going to be the next US Senator from Hawaii."

10

"Mrs. Matisse?"

Christel looked up from her desk and immediately melted into a wide smile. "Well, hello there Mr. Matisse." She clicked out of her accounting software program and closed her laptop. Grinning, she stood and held up her hand, admiring her wedding ring. "I still can't believe I'm your wife."

Evan pulled her into his arms. "You still owe me that honeymoon," he whispered against her ear.

She leaned back, enjoying the kisses he brushed against her neck. "I—I'm sorry I'm so busy," she said, breathless. "Your proposal came as a surprise. So did the ceremony. I—" She paused, enjoying the way his lips felt against her skin. "I promise we'll get away soon."

She felt his hand in her hair. "We'll just have to practice until then." His mouth found hers and Christel closed her eyes, enjoying the taste of him, the feel of him pressed against her.

Someone cleared their throat from the doorway. "Get a room, you two!"

Christel pulled back to find her sister standing just inside the door with her hands on her hips and an amused look on her face.

"I'm sorry, am I interrupting?" Katie grinned. "Clearly, I came at a wrong time."

"What do you need?" Christel asked, her voice filled with annoyance.

Katie glanced around Christel's office. "I think we could redo your office to include a trundle bed for the newlyweds. There's plenty of room."

Evan laughed. "I wouldn't argue against that. So long as a lock is added to the door," he teased.

Christel shook her head. "Stop. Both of you." Nonplussed, she directed her full attention to her sister. "What did you need?"

"I needed to talk to you about something." She glanced between Christel and Evan. "But I can come back a little later."

Evan lifted his hand. "No, stay. I was on my way to the hospital and just dropped by to say hi...to my new wife." He looked over at Christel like he couldn't seem to get enough of her. "But I have a surgery in a couple of hours and need to get going." He turned to Christel. "So, I'll see you at home tonight?"

She smiled and winked at him. "See you at home."

Evan brushed her cheek with a kiss and headed out the door. Christel then motioned to her guest chair, still smiling. "Sit. What do you need?"

Katie sat and started picking lint off her pants. "I need to tell you something."

Christel placed her clasped hands on the top of her desk and steepled her fingers. "I'm listening."

Katie opened her mouth but before she could speak Christel's phone rang. She held up a finger. "Sorry. Hold that thought."

The call was from an OSHA representative who had a question about an accident report they'd filed after a worker mistakenly walked straight into one of the electric fences meant to keep out feral pigs. The fact he was standing in a small puddle of water magnified the shock.

Christel had the foresight to anticipate this call and had conducted a good measure of legal research as to what ramifications Pali Maui might expect. In the end, the representative simply needed to be assured corrective measures had been instituted and were in place to keep a similar incident from occurring in the future. Thanks to Mig's idea, the current to their fencing would be cut anytime workers were in the area. It wasn't likely feral pigs would breach the perimeter when people were nearby. Most of the incidents occurred at night, when the pigs rooted for food.

When the call ended, Christel looked up to find Katie gone. She shrugged and opened her laptop. No doubt her sister would return...if it was important.

KATIE GROANED. What she needed to tell Christel was extremely important. She desperately needed to warn her sister about Greer Latham and come clean about what had happened. She'd been foolish to think she'd have her sister's uninterrupted attention while Christel was at work. Katie would simply have to catch her later.

Admittedly, she didn't relish revealing the real reason why her trip to Honolulu months ago had gone down in flames—about how her manufacturing proposal for a project she had dreamed up had hit a wall. She'd have to answer why she didn't tell anyone about the ill-fated incident with Greer Latham... especially Jon.

While she didn't have a great answer for keeping what had happened on her trip secret, she remembered Christel was already against proceeding with the proposal, stating the timing was off. It was simply too close after their father had died. She urged Katie to put her idea to expand the gift shop and introduce new product lines on hold until Christel had more time to focus on the situation. The fact was, Christel didn't think she was up for the job without her help.

Katie also knew her sister and mom hoped to redesign the golf course soon. The renovation project would take precedence and any extra capital or use of credit lines, would be directed there.

Ignoring all that, Katie had hoped that she could put the deal together on her own, one with financial terms no one could balk at. And her idea had been a good one. The meeting went well and concluded with a promise of funding, just like she'd hoped. The only problem she encountered was Greer Latham. Unfortunately, she'd learned he was a sleazeball.

Katie shuddered remembering how he'd slipped his hand onto her leg suggestively on the way to the airport. He had more in mind than extending a loan, that was apparent.

What was Jon going to say when he found out?

They had just weathered a marital storm and now she was about to send their relationship headlong into another squall, one with potential gale force winds.

Katie had tossed and turned all last night pondering how to avoid coming clean. Truth was, she couldn't—not now. Not when Pali Maui was at stake.

Katie straightened her shoulders and drew a deep breath. She couldn't put this off any longer. If Christel was busy, she needed to go talk to Jon before he got swept up with the lunch crowd. If she told him now, he might have time to cool off before getting home this evening.

She found her husband over at the restaurant in the kitchen going over payroll and attendance records, a task that would already have him in a foul mood. How many times had Jon complained that his wait staff was notorious for showing up for work late but expected to be paid for the missed time?

"Honey, do you have a minute?"

Jon barely looked up. "What do you need, babe?"

"I need to talk to you." When his attention remained on the paperwork, she added, "It's important."

Jon held up an open palm. "Just a minute."

Katie waited impatiently for several seconds before she'd had enough. "Jon! I said we need to talk."

Jon slowly raised his head and looked her way. "What is it?"

"Could we go outside a minute?" She pointed to the deck.

He wiped his hands on a kitchen towel. "Sure, but I can't be long."

Katie headed for the deck and leaned her elbows on the railing, letting the vista buoy her spirits. Before she could bail on her intention, she opened her mouth and began telling Jon about her trip.

"You remember when I took that business trip to Honolulu and you picked me up at the airport?"

His face broke into a smile. "Yeah, I remember. I picked you up thinking you were pregnant."

Katie joined him in the memory. "Oh, yeah. I remember. Upon learning the truth, that the pregnancy test you'd found in the trash was not mine, we both immediately assumed it belonged to Willa."

Jon leaned his elbows over the deck and looked out over the golf course. "Thank goodness we were wrong...on both counts."

Katie knew that was her moment. "Well, there was something I'd intended to tell you but didn't because of all that distraction. I mean, immediately we were focused on our daughter."

Jon looked at her. "Yeah?"

"Well, what I didn't tell you was that the guy I met with offered to take me to the airport. On the way, he made a play."

Jon scowled. "What do you mean...a play?"

She told him how Greer Latham had suggested they were each lonely and might *meet each other's needs*. "I immediately set him straight, of course."

Jon looked, his expression a mixture of puzzlement and anger. "Why are you telling me all this now?"

Katie chewed at her lip. "Because Mom and Christel have agreed to a bridge loan with Latham Enterprises to finance the golf course renovation."

11

Aiden finished filling out the incident report for yesterday's successful search and rescue of two lost hikers when they went off trail near Haleakala National Park. One of the things he'd never expected when he was promoted to captain here at Maui Emergency Services was how much paperwork the job required.

He signed his name on the designated line and placed the report on top of the stack of papers on his desk. A quick glance at the wall clock reminded him why his stomach was growling. He'd neglected to eat lunch and it was nearly time for dinner.

He grabbed his jacket off the back of his office chair. The rest of the paperwork would wait until tomorrow.

On his way out, he passed the door to his former office where he worked prior to his promotion. He peeked inside to find Meghan sitting with her feet up on the desk. She was eating a microwaved slice of frozen pizza.

"Mmm...another gourmet dinner, I see." Aiden grinned at her as he slipped his arms inside his jacket.

She smiled back. "Heading out early again, I see," she teased. "Where do I find one of those cushy management jobs."

They both knew the two of them were perhaps the hardest working individuals on the team. Rarely did either of them only put in an eight-hour day. More like twelve to fourteen.

Meghan held up her mostly-eaten slice of pizza. "Want some?"

Aiden shook his head. "Nah. As tempting as it is to eat your left-overs, I'm meeting my brother and Ori Kané for dinner."

"Ah, a social life. I remember that." Meghan shoved the remaining slice into her mouth leaving sauce clinging to her lips.

Aiden stared. How could a girl as beautiful as Meghan act so much like one of the guys? Okay, yeah. He was in management now and shouldn't notice what she looked like. Even so, he was human. Off the record, he knew her to be tough as nails. She was also incredibly attractive.

He was a little surprised that Shane agreed to meet at the restaurant where he'd met Aimee. Surely, the wounds of her leaving him remained fresh. Especially since he was the one left pulling baby duty. Aiden had to say, his younger brother had really stepped up to the plate there. He worked and took care of Carson declining help from their mom and sisters. Who would have guessed he had it in him?

Charley's was located in Pa'ia a short distance from their favorite ball field and was a popular bar and restaurant named after a Great Dane dog and where gray-bearded bikers and young surfers both lined up for the best food and fun around. Willie Nelson claimed Charley's was his kind of place and often played impromptu concerts on the tiny stage anytime he visited the island.

Ori and Shane were already seated at a corner booth at the rear of the bustling establishment. Baby Carson was asleep in a carry-all, his little thumb tucked inside his tiny lips.

"Hey, guys." Aiden slipped onto the vinyl seat next to Ori. "Sorry I'm late."

"You're right on time," Shane reported. "We know you'll be late so we always tell you to be here fifteen minutes before the real time we want to meet."

Ori elbowed Shane. "Shh...don't tell our secret. Now he'll show up late for real."

A middle-aged waitress appeared with an order pad and pen. "Hey, what can I get for you, boys?" She turned her eyes on Shane, then at the sleeping baby, and smiled.

She took their orders: beers and hamburgers with all the fixings, including extra onions on Shane's.

"What?" he said when Aiden stared at him. "That's what they make breath mints for."

After catching up for a few minutes, Ori leaned back in his seat. "So, as great as it is to get all the updates, I asked you guys out to lunch for a reason."

Aiden took a drink from his frosted mug. "Yeah? What's that?"

"As you know, the center is bulging at the seams, in terms of people showing up for help."

Right out of college, Ori helped start *Ka Hale a Ke Ola* Resource Center, an outreach that served hundreds of meals to elderly and needy individuals each week. In recent years, the center had expanded and now was also known for finding housing, used cars, and jobs, as well as providing employment training. If someone needed it, Ori worked to make it happen.

Aiden leaned and reached in his back pocket for his wallet.

Ori quickly waved him off. "I'll never turn down donations, but I'm not talking about money."

Shane looked over at Carson, checking on him. "What are you talking?"

Ori gave them both a wide smile. "I've got some kids, mainly boys, who desperately need some mentoring. But not in the typical sense. I'm thinking of starting up a baseball team. Many of these kids don't have dads to teach them to field a ball, to pitch, or even what teamwork really means." He looked across the table at his buddies. "That's where you come in."

Shane lifted a brow. "What do you mean?"

"I mean, I want you guys to coach. We had far more kids interested than I can fit on one team. I want you two to coach a second team."

Aiden lifted a hundred dollar bill and slid it across at Ori who tucked it in his pocket and thanked him for the donation.

"So, what do you say? Are you guys in?" Ori waited for their response.

Shane and Aiden exchanged glances. "I dunno," Aiden said. "Shane's got a kid."

"He can bring the baby to the games," Ori assured. "There'll always be someone who can keep an eye on him. Likely, he'll be fawned all over and spoiled rotten."

"I'm in," Shane announced, not giving the notion a second thought.

Aiden raised his eyebrows. "That was fast."

"It's for a good cause," his brother quickly noted.

On second thought, coaching might provide a much-needed distraction for Shane. He shrugged. "Okay, I guess you can include me as well."

Ori's expression brightened. "Great. I knew you guys would help out!"

Suddenly, Shane's attention was diverted.

Aiden looked to see a tall girl with long brown hair pulled into a ponytail. She wore a sheer swim cover-up that barely hid the bikini underneath.

Shane caught Aiden watching. "What? I got dumped. I'm not dead."

12

"What? Why didn't you tell us?" Christel demanded.

Katie's mother lifted her hand to her mouth. She shook her head. "Oh, honey. Yes, why didn't you say something?"

Christel parked her open palms on her mom's kitchen island, leaned and glared at Katie who sat in a barstool opposite her. "Your timing sucks! Everything is signed. We can't just back out of our loan agreement."

Katie fought tears. "I know, I know. I should have said something earlier. I was...well, the entire situation was embarrassing." She refrained from saying she didn't relish her sister knowing she hadn't been able to bring home a successful manufacturing deal, and why. Christel would never have gotten herself in a situation like that.

Christel reluctantly turned her attention away from her sister and focused on her mom. "What now, Mom? This guy sounds like a real jerk."

Ava paced the kitchen floor for several seconds. As was her habit, she chewed on her knuckle while thinking. Suddenly, she stopped and turned to face her girls. "Okay, let's take a breath. Think this through rationally and come up with a plan."

"I'm sorry. I really am. I should have said something back then." Katie traced the pattern in the granite with her finger. "Jon says we should confront the situation up front. He wants to put Greer Latham on notice that no future breech of propriety will be tolerated."

Christel huffed. "That's a husband talking, not a business partner. Latham, our financing partner, is not someone we can afford to push away."

Katie let her expression grow determined. "Are we? Partners with Greer Latham?"

Ava lightly rubbed Katie's back. "Honey, had we known, we'd never have entertained doing business with someone like that. Unfortunately, we're now under contract and while we're not partners in the general sense, when a company obtains financing, the company is subject to the lender in many ways." She said this like she was explaining simple business concepts to a child, which irked Katie to no end. She might have messed up a little, but she wasn't stupid. She single-handedly built and arranged financing for an expensive home. Yes, this renovation was on a much larger scale, but the basic concepts were the same, weren't they?

Her mother continued her clarification. "Thankfully, a bridge loan is short-term and only in place until the project is completed and permanent financing is in place. Even so, our contract includes provisions that may not be in our best interest, should we encounter unexpected delays. A good relationship with our lenders is essential. No one likes to be vulnerable to unscrupulous individuals. Unfortunately, we already are." Her mother paused. "Damage control is essential here. Do you understand?"

Katie didn't bother hiding her annoyance. Of course, she

understood. Did they forget she was the victim here and that she'd immediately bailed from the car that day? She swallowed her wounded pride and took a deep breath, hoping for a solution. "His mother seemed to be all business. Sylvia was definitely on the up-and-up."

"Sylvia? You are on a first name basis with the CEO of Latham Enterprises?" Christel groaned. "I knew I should have attended that meeting with you, especially when you wouldn't take my advice and wait for better timing. Now look where we're at."

"Look at where we're at? You're the one who pushed forward with financing for this project without asking any of the rest of the family for their thoughts and opinions. You left me out." She stubbornly lifted her chin. "Besides, you think I invited his advances? I promise you this...I did not!"

Katie's mom raised her hands. "Okay, the blame game doesn't further our business goals. Christel, let's focus."

Katie suppressed a grin. That was the closest to a reprimand she'd ever heard her mother direct at her sister.

Not leaving the issue alone, Christel continued. "So, how exactly did you leave all this? Besides exiting the car, I mean?"

This is where Katie strongly considered holding back information. Yet, that approach is the very one that had gotten her into this trouble. She took a deep breath realizing she had to come completely clean. "I think I called him a barf bucket."

Christel rolled her eyes and waved her hands. "Oh, great! Just great. You called our lender a barf bucket." She looked at her mother. "Is there any guess as to how this renovation project is going to go?"

Ava held up open palms. "Okay, here's the deal. I will call this woman...what was her name?"

"Sylvia Latham," Katie offered.

"Sylvia. Okay, I will call her and set up a meeting. Both of you girls will attend with me as well as Tom Strobe, the golf course architect we'll be working with. The purpose of the meeting will be to introduce Tom and his plans and answer any questions they may still have. This meeting will also provide an opportunity for us to assess the climate and establish rapport."

Christel nodded and rubbed open palms. "Yes, that's a good plan. I like it."

Katie groaned inside. "I have to go?"

Christel gave her a stark look. "Of course you have to go. How else will we be able to tell how Greer Latham and his mother are going to react going forward?"

"His mother could be unaware of her son's breech," her mom suggested. She placed her hand on Katie's shoulder. "Just for the record, I'm proud of the way you let this creep have it." She glanced over at Christel. "It's only unfortunate we were left in the dark."

13

Christel tossed the remainder of her coffee in the sink and stole another glance at her watch. Evan came up behind her, folded his arms around her and buried his face against her neck. "I'm not opposed to sneaking back to bed. What do you say?"

"I say, I'd love to. Unfortunately, I have a plane to catch."

He nuzzled her neck with his nose. "Take the next flight. I have an orthoscopic knee replacement, but the surgery doesn't start until the doc shows up."

"Ah...so that explains the long wait times in doctors' offices."

Evan laughed. "Yes, all the medical professionals are home having wild romantic interludes with their new spouses."

Christel turned, grinning. "Please tell me I can have a raincheck. My return flight is scheduled to land at 9:30 p.m. If I hurry, I can be home by 10:00."

He reluctantly released her. "I'll be undressed and waiting for you beneath the sheets. Don't be late," he playfully warned.

Christel smiled. She had forgotten how much she loved

being married. It had been so long since another toothbrush had hung next to hers in her bathroom, a man's slippers lay next to hers in the closet, or she'd felt the warmth of a body against her in bed. She loved reaching over and touching her new husband's warm chest beside her and listening to him breathe while he slept.

On the outside, she was hardworking, educated, and qualified. No doubt, she could easily take care of herself in every way, especially financially. On the inside, she intimately longed to share this human experience with a lifelong committed partner who adored her. She was meant to be married.

When she got home tonight, she intended to make sure her new husband knew how happy he made her.

Christel arrived at the airport with a well-packed Kate Spade business tote over her shoulder. There was no telling what topic might come up in the meeting and she wanted to be prepared to answer to any questions raised. Her mother said repeatedly that this trip was primarily to cement a good relationship with their short-term lenders, especially since Katie revealed there was a hidden crack in the sidewalk, one they all hoped would not trip up this project.

Despite her mother's main focus, Christel wanted to make certain that Latham Enterprises had no financial reason to doubt their decision to extend funds for Pali Maui's golf course renovation. Everything needed to go according to plan in order to finish construction and put permanent financing in place.

Professionals did not allow emotions to dictate the course of business decisions. From what she'd read, Sylvia Latham was someone who was all business, highly respected and known to be a major player in the financial industry. According to the internet, Sylvia had attended the Allen and Company business forum in Sun Valley, Idaho—an invite-only event open to only the top one percent in the business community with attendees like Jeff Bezos and Warren Buffet. Yes, Sylvia Latham ran in *those* circles.

Beyond this project, someone with those resources would be good to have in your back business pocket, so to speak.

"Honey," her mother's voice called out. "Over here."

Christel searched the crowd gathered at boarding. Finally, she spotted her mom standing beside Katie, waving.

"You're late," Katie accused as Christel joined them. She shoved a grande Starbuck's cup into her hand. "A caramel macchiato with extra espresso."

Christel gratefully accepted. "If this is intended to be a peace offering, don't think a coffee drink gets you off the hook."

"Of course not," Katie conceded. "We all know you intend to keep me dangling from that proverbial hook for at least a few months."

Ava gave them both a look. "Enough, you two." She stepped forward in the line, fished out her phone and scrolled to her digital boarding pass."

Christel glanced around. "Where's Tom Strobe?"

Her mother waited for the airline steward to swipe her phone. "He'll meet us over there. He had some business in Honolulu and flew out last night."

Christel nodded and handed over her phone to be swiped. "Is he aware of the...situation?"

"No, I didn't think it necessary to widen the circle." Ava pasted a wide smile on her face. "Besides, everything is going to go just fine. You'll see."

Christel wanted to believe her mother. A still small voice reminded how her mom always saw the cup half full, even when the glass had a large crack. It was only in the past few months that Christel had secretly allowed herself to evaluate the situation with her father more closely. Had her mother seen signs of his infidelity and looked the other way? If he hadn't died in that accident, would they even have known about his affair with Mia?

It would hardly matter now except that she often wondered if that trait in her mother had somehow sifted over into her own life. Is that why she refused to acknowledge how bad Jay's addiction had become prior to the divorce?

She drew a deep breath and forced herself to let go of those thoughts. At least in this case, her mother's optimism might have an upside. Christel lifted her chin slightly. While she didn't want to refuse to see the truth, she couldn't let others' actions knock her off course and take her under.

Right now, she only had one focus. She couldn't let this meeting go badly.

Sylvia Latham stood from her seat at the head of the large granite conference table when they entered her board room. "Welcome!" She greeted each of them with a firm handshake. "It was so good of you to ask for this meeting, Ava." She paused. "I hope you agree that we can set aside formalities and go with first names?"

"Of course," Ava said warmly. "And thank you for agreeing to meet."

A quick glance around the room revealed Greer Latham was not present. Christel could visibly see her sister's shoulders relax.

Introductions were made. Ava turned to Tom Strobe. "This is the star of the show, our architect."

Sylvia's stern features broke into a smile. She fingered the pearls at her neck. "You have an impressive background, Mr. Strobe."

"Tom. We're on first name basis in this meeting," he reminded with his own wide smile.

"Of course," Sylvia said as she pointed to a coffee cart near the massive glass windows overlooking the Waikiki shoreline. "Can I get any of you something to drink?" She lifted a delicate cup emblazoned with the Latham Enterprises logo.

In unison, they all declined. At Sylvia's invitation, they took seats around the table.

"I apologize. My son, Greer, has been held up with another matter. He will be joining us shortly."

Christel kept her face from reacting to the news, as did Katie. Their mother simply nodded. "I'm anxious to meet him."

"Greer has wonderful things to say about your operation," Sylvia reported. "He is hard to impress, so count that as a compliment." It was then she looked across at Katie. Her brows drew together slightly. "We've met before, haven't we?"

Katie swallowed. "Yes. We had a meeting a few months back about a manufacturing agreement."

Sylvia's face brightened. She nodded as she filled her cup with coffee from a large silver urn. "Oh, yes. I remember. I was saddened to learn you had changed directions."

Christel's heart pounded. This was a point when things could sour.

"We still hope to proceed. Unfortunately, the timing was off." Katie kept her poker face in place. "Especially with the golf course renovation on the horizon."

Christel knew her sister well enough to know she was barely breathing.

"Ah, that is good to hear." Sylvia returned to her place at the head of the table. "Then I'm hopeful we can revisit the project, when the timing is better."

Christel let out the breath she'd been holding. So far, so good.

The conference room door opened and in strode a man with thick, sandy-colored hair, cut to precision. He wore a tailored suit with shoes she knew to be Berlutis. Their eyes met as he eased the door closed.

"Sorry I'm late," he said, pulling on his crisp shirt cuffs. "The delay couldn't be avoided." His eyes roamed the people around the table, landing on Katie. "Hello, Ms. Ackerman. Nice to see you again."

His face broke into a smile as he moved to the empty chair next to her.

Christel frowned. *Not good. Not good at all.*

His mother made introductions, taking several minutes to again highlight Tom Strobe's professional accolades.

Greer Lathan barely acknowledged Tom. He simply nodded in his mother's direction.

Sylvia fingered a silver-haired curl at the back of her neck. "This is our first golf project. We're very pleased to financially partner with Pali Maui."

Katie kept her sight trained outside the ceiling-to-floor windows overlooking Waikiki Beach. Christel drew a deep breath and turned her attention to the plush carpet, with its leaf design in shades of teal and cream.

Ava leaned over the table and steepled her fingers. "We feel exactly the same, Sylvia."

Christel bent to her bag and withdrew sealed manila envelopes. She stood and passed the packages to the meeting participants. "You will see that our forecasts have been updated, much in our favor."

Tom nodded. "We now believe we will see a considerable reduction in landscaping costs based on our new agreement with a commercial landscaper located on Maui. The local nature will eliminate shipment costs and contractor expenses."

Christel exchanged glances with her mother. The meeting was going well. Much better than expected.

She felt herself relax when, across the table, Katie's face

grew as stoic as cement. Next to her, a tiny smile nipped at the corners of Greer Latham's mouth.

Christel couldn't keep a scowl from forming. She mumbled something about more information and ducked to her tote, pretending to retrieve more envelopes. That's when she saw it.

That creep had his hand on her sister's leg.

Christel straightened and glared across the table. Greer Latham took note and smiled ever so slightly more, almost as if he enjoyed the fact that she knew.

She glanced over at her mother who was in deep conversation with Sylvia and Tom, something about the cost of putting greens. She turned and glared at Greer.

Katie remained still. She was electing to not react!

Christel stood and pounded the table with her fist. The action immediately drew everyone's attention.

"Christel?" her mom questioned.

"That's it!" Christel marched around the table and gathered the packages, even pulling a schematic right out of Sylvia's hand. "We're done!"

Christel watched Sylvia. Nothing on the face of the silver-haired woman gave a clue as to her reaction. That 'ole witch in her four-thousand-dollar Valentino suit knew…she knew full well her son was a lecherous creep. And she stood by and said nothing.

Well, she would say something!

She motioned to her sister. "C'mon, we're leaving."

Katie raised her eyebrows in surprise. "Are you sure?"

"Oh, I'm sure." Christel jabbed a finger in the air in Greer Latham's direction. "You, sir, are a reprobate swine. How dare you put my sister in such an uncomfortable position? Twice! Surely you do not believe Pali Maui needs financing to such a degree that we will all look the other way while you fondle Katie's leg?"

Greer Latham stood. He looked at his mother. "I believe this partnership might not be in our interests after all."

She nodded as she stood and grabbed the conference phone on the table. She pursed her lips and pressed a button. "Get legal on the phone."

Christel huffed. "News flash! You're looking at Pali Maui's legal department right now. I'm not certain you want to press me on this issue and hold us to the contract. In addition to enforcing any legal remedies, I will pursue every other means at my disposal. Did you know my mother's sister was the former lead anchor of a major news station in Seattle? I'm sure she wouldn't mind making a quick telephone call to her former coworkers. Of course, news like that will quickly spread, especially on social media."

She stared directly at Greer this time. "Given your son's wandering hands, we will use everything in our arsenal to make his improprieties public. I'm sure both national and local media would be very interested in another salacious #MeToo story involving one of the biggest financial players in Hawaii." Christel turned to Sylvia and leaned in close. "Do I need to remind you how that worked out for Charlie Rose? How he was axed from the Allen & Company conference in Sun Valley? It would be a pity if you weren't included on the invite list next summer."

That seemed to be the tip that toppled her. Sylvia slowly withdrew her hand from the button. "Katherine, cancel that."

Christel dared to look over at her mother, who thankfully gave her an affirmative nod. Even Tom Strobe seemed not only surprised by the turn of events, but pleased with Christel's position.

Most of all, Katie appreciated the support, evidenced by the tears forming in her eyes. Christel quickly moved to her side and placed her arm around her sister's shoulders. "C'mon, Katie. Let's get out of here."

They gathered their things and made their way out of the conference room as quickly as possible, not bothering to look back. It wasn't until the elevator doors slid shut that Christel turned to the rest of them.

"Well, now what?"

14

"He did what!?" Alani parked her hands on her ample hips and glared. "Christel was right to tell those Latham people to take a flying leap. That evil playboy better not ever show his face at one of my luaus. He may end up in the pork pit, roasting with the other pigs."

Ava sighed and nodded in agreement. "It was a mistake for me to try to salvage a bad situation. Frankly, my instincts told me to run from Latham Enterprises. I simply didn't know how to extract our company from the agreement we'd entered into without severe legal and financial ramifications." She let out a slight chuckle. "Of course, Christel took care of that."

A smile formed creating dimples at either side of Alani's plump cheeks. "I wish I could have been there to see it. There was a time I prayed and prayed for Christel to grow some backbone and deal with that addicted husband of hers." She shook her head as she followed Ava up into the baseball stands. "She enabled him to get away with far too much. Now, I'm not advocating for divorce. In God's eyes, marriage is forever. Still, the fact she finally had enough and formed firm boundaries was divine intervention. At least in my mind."

The Last Aloha

Ava swept off the metal seat with her hand and sat. "Yes, my daughter can get fired up...in the right situation. She's very protective of her family."

Alani maneuvered into the space beside Ava. "So, what are you going to do now? I mean, about the financing."

Ava let out a heavy sigh. "I truly don't know. I suppose we're going to have to put the renovation on hold until we can secure short-term financing. The worst thing about that is Tom Strobe is highly sought after. He's likely to get pulled onto another project very soon. Time is of the essence here."

Alani patted her leg. "God has a way of making all things work out."

Ava considered how her best friend continued to remain positive in all situations. Her faith grounded her, she supposed. Alani always looked for the good in every situation and in every person, even to the point of being quick to forgive when Mia broke her heart last year. Ava knew Alani struggled with her daughter's choices and how they created a ripple effect of pain and hurt. Even so, she extended grace.

Ava could fully understand Alani's love for her daughter. If any of her own children were in a similar situation, Ava knew her love would surpass anything they had done.

However, that affection did not extend to her dead husband. She had made a decision to focus on joy in the aftermath of his betrayal, but she would never forgive Lincoln for having an affair with her best friend's daughter.

"Speaking of your girls," Alani said. "Where are they?"

Ava pointed to the concession stand. "Ori talked them into working. Jon is watching Carson and Noelle while Christel and Katie are selling items that were baked and donated by Halia Aka and the girls at the Banana Patch. Katie even roped Willa into helping out. Her teenaged protests hit a complete wall when Katie argued it was for a good cause."

Alani puffed up with pride. "Yes, Ori has a servant's heart, that's for certain. When there is a need, he moved heaven and earth to fill it. And if the need involves children? Well, he's not opposed to pressuring everyone he knows to come along and help him. He'd hand Jesus Himself an apron if there were hungry kids to be fed."

Ava let out a slight laugh. "I'm not sure my granddaughter's motives are as pure. I highly suspect there may have been a little bribery involved. Willa is wanting to learn to drive, and Katie is utilizing the situation to her benefit at every opportunity."

"Hey, you two!"

Ava turned to see her sister climbing the stands and heading for them. She wore a tight-fitting T-shirt emblazoned with the slogan, "Jim Kahele: Your Choice for Change." "I'm a little late. Did I miss anything?"

Ava shook her head and pointed out to the ball field. "No, the first inning is just starting."

Vanessa slipped in beside them. "I love this cause. She pulled her phone out of her back jeans pocket and started thumbing a note. Jim needs to get involved in this."

Ava frowned. "Oh, I don't think—"

Alani placed her hand on Ava's arm. "That's a wonderful idea," she said. "Of course, I'm sure Mr. Kahele would be happy to make a substantial donation to Ka Hale a Ke Ola Resource Center. Ori is grateful for every dollar. These kids deserve our support."

Vanessa grinned while adding to the note on her phone. "I'm sure that can be arranged."

"How is all that going?" Alani asked. "I mean, with the campaign and all."

Vanessa closed down her phone and placed it in her lap. "Wonderfully. We have a new campaign slogan." She pointed to her shirt.

"I see that," Ava remarked.

"I hired a designer I worked with in Seattle," Vanessa continued. "She developed an amazing logo which targets our primary voting demographic. The design incorporates two comment windows above Jim's name with a bold red arrow running through them." She turned to show them the logo on the reverse side of her shirt. "The visual message signals that communication is important to Jim and he will create change based on what his constituents care about. I ran both the logo and slogan through several focus groups. Spot on!"

Vanessa shielded her eyes from the sun. "Hawaii is hungry for enlightened leadership—leadership that empowers the people's voice and that facilitates collaboration and problem solving. Leadership that can implement and move forward real solutions. In fact, I've arranged for Jim to engage with voters in a bi-weekly Q&A called *Kahele Listens*. The first episode will be held as a livestream on social media. Each broadcast will address a specific topic, with the first focusing on the importance of protecting our precious ecosystem while still opening new doors to commerce."

Her face was beaming. "This job is perfect for me, even if I do say so myself." Her sister gave a brief look at Ava daring her to challenge the assertion.

Ava had long since moved past Vanessa and her career woes. She had more important things to think about—new financing being at the top of that list. Of course, that would have to wait. Right now, she had a ballgame to support.

Out in the field, Shane and Aiden herded a team of young boys and girls out of the makeshift dugout and onto the field. Thanks to a generous donation from Pali Maui, they all wore new uniforms and protective gear.

"Batter up!" the referee shouted.

Only minutes into the first inning, a vocal parent sitting behind them stood and yelled. Ava turned to see a petite woman dressed in white jeans, light pink shirt with a matching head scarf holding a megaphone to her mouth. "Quit being a wimp," she screamed. "Kill 'em...get that uniform dirty!"

Maybe it was Ava's age, or maybe the stress she'd been under when the financial deal folded, but she sincerely had no patience. She found herself wanting to drag that tiny woman behind the portable outhouse and plug some toilet paper in her mouth.

Alani gave her a nudge. "You're having unholy thoughts."

Ava rolled her eyes. "Says who?"

"Says the look on that face of yours."

Ava couldn't help it. She burst into laughter.

Wasn't that exactly what best friends were for? To call you on your junk and do it with a smile?

KATIE LIGHTLY JABBED her elbow into Willa. "Heads-up... honey. It's the seventh-inning-stretch. It's about to get busy."

Willa groaned inside. She didn't want to be here in the first place. What if someone she knew saw her in this silly white apron her mom had forced on her?

Just as the thought formed, she spotted a boy standing in line that she'd never seen before. It was possible he was a student at her school but she doubted it. She might not know everyone's names but she at least knew faces.

He spotted her too, and smiled.

Willa nearly dropped the cupcake she'd been bagging.

"Careful, Willa," her mom warned. "Pay attention to what you're doing."

Ugh. That's all she needed...her mother scolding her in front of the cute guy in line. Actually, cute didn't even start to describe him. First, he had blond hair that hung just over his ears and swept onto his forehead. He was tall, and even from here, she could see he was athletic. Mostly, she loved the way dimples formed when he smiled at her.

"Hey," he said as he stepped up to the counter. "I hear you have awesome cupcakes."

Willa cleared her throat trying to find her voice. "Uh, yeah. We do. Alani Kané made them. She's my Gramma Ava's best friend. They've known each other for years."

He looked at her and shrugged. "Great. Can I have one?"

Willa groaned inside. Why did she have to ramble?

She quickly grabbed the tray. "There are several kinds," she offered.

The boy smiled at her. There were those dimples again. "Which do you recommend?"

Willa smiled back. "Oh, the pineapple coconut. The frosting is amazing."

He took his wallet out of the back pocket of his uniform. "Sold." He handed her a bill.

Willa struggled to calculate the proper change when a noise from across the field caught her attention.

"Eh...batter, batter, batter!" The blond-haired woman jumped up and down on the stands sending her chest bouncing.

The kid turned to check it out too. "Wow. Who's that?"

Willa lifted her hand shaded her eyes to get a better look. "Oh, her? That's Wimberly Ann. She's a realtor who sold my Uncle Shane his house. Looks like she's here with Mig, our operations manager at Pali Maui. I overheard my mom say they're becoming a thing."

The boy smiled. "Well, she sure is enthusiastic. Someone might tell her that we're between innings. The kid out there throwing the ball across the plate is only practicing."

Willa laughed.

"You mentioned Pali Maui. You related to Aiden?" He nodded toward the field.

She nodded. "My uncle." She handed him his change, then slid a small paper plate with the cupcake on it into his hand. "He's helping out Ori with this team. My other uncle, Shane, is coaching the grade school aged kids. They play right after this game."

"Oh, Ori's great! So are both your uncles. Good guys."

Willa wanted to ask him what position he played, how long he'd played, where he went to school...a million questions. Before either of them could say more, her mom looked over at her from down the counter where she was taking an order. She scowled and pointed to the long line of people waiting in front of Willa.

"Oh, I guess I'd better..." Willa pointed behind him.

He quickly nodded. "Yeah, gotcha." He started to go, then paused. "Hey, what's your name?"

Willa's face broke into a wide grin. "Willa...Willa Ackerman."

"I'm Devon Connor." Seeming reluctant, he finally took a step back. "Okay, yeah. See you around, Willa Ackerman." He held up the plate. "And thanks for the cupcake."

As soon as he jogged away, a woman with three little kids approached. "I don't suppose you have Dole Whip?" she asked.

Willa answered, but kept her eyes on Devon as he returned to the game. Only one more half inning and then Shane's team would play. After that, she was done and free to head home.

The first thing she planned to do was to call Kina, her best friend, and tell her all about the new guy she'd met at the ballgame.

15

Ava and Christel huddled around a stack of documents on Christel's desk. "Let me see the cash projections again." Ava held out her hand.

Christel rifled through the stack and held out a stapled report. "Here. But it's not going to say anything different than what I've been telling you. We have a couple of very limited options. Even then, I'm not sure the strategies would produce enough capital to move forward with the renovation without a loan."

Ava scanned the document, flipped to the second page. "Yes, but that means a major delay and loss of Tom Strobe." She kept her eyes trained on the monthly income projections, hoping to hide the fact that her wanting Tom to remain on the project extended past pure business reasons. She liked him. Only as a friend, of course. Lincoln had been dead only a little over a year and it was far too soon to think about another romantic relationship, if she ever would. Still, she enjoyed Tom's friendship. The few times they'd been together had been enjoyable with interesting conversation that did not revolve around her kids and their busy lives.

Surprisingly, she learned he liked art. This prompted her to show him the commissioned oil piece that hung in her living room—a Danielle Nelisse, a local artist she adored. Her work was expressive, modern, and dramatic. Tom admired the abstract piece as much as she and claimed the wide sweeps of bright color were filled with emotion.

"Did you know her work was showcased in *Artist Talk* magazine in London?" he had asked leaning in closer for a better look.

It would be a shame to lose his help on this project.

Christel ran a hand through her two-tier choppy bob, a haircut Ava knew cost her daughter a pretty penny to maintain. "Mom, the only thing I can offer is to start asking for cash up front from some of our slow pays." She pointed out a couple of line items on the document Ava was reviewing. "Or, we could structure receivables to include discounts for early payments on bulk shipments."

Ava shook her head. "No, that's not an option. We already face heavy competition with the pineapple operations in Costa Rica who run at much less overhead than we do in the States. If we don't continue the payment options we currently have in place, we'll likely lose some key accounts. That defeats our purpose."

The door opened and Mig stood just inside, holding his cap in his hand. "Uh, I hope I'm not interrupting," he said as he waited to be invited in.

Ava waved for him to join them. "You're never interrupting, Mig. What do you need?"

His face grew somber. "Would you mind sitting? I have something important I want to talk to you about."

Ava couldn't help it. Her heart sped up a little. It was unusual for Mig to be so serious. Oh, goodness. She hoped this didn't have anything to do with that realtor woman he was seeing.

They sat at the small round conference table in the corner of Christel's office. Mig placed his cap on the table in front of him. "This morning, Katie told me about the meeting."

Ava nodded. "Yes, things could have gone better. Still, I think we're good to be rid of any affiliation with Greer Latham and his mother. I should have listened to my gut early on." She used to trust her instincts, that is until Lincoln's affair came to light. She now worried she only saw what she really wanted to see. She doubted herself and her decisions.

"Well, that's what I want to talk to you about." Mig took a deep breath. "And I want you both to hear me out before reacting."

Ava and Christel exchanged glances.

"I have money," he began. "And I want to offer it to you."

Ava quickly held up two open palms. "Oh, no." She shook her head. "That would never be a consideration."

"Just hear me out, Ava." His voice was a bit stern. "You have said yourself that I have been a part of Pali Maui for so many years that I might as well be part of the family. Well, I feel like part of the family. Family helps family when needed."

She opened her mouth to say something more. He stopped her.

"It will hurt me deeply if you say no to my offer. Like I said, I have money. Pali Maui is very generous with my salary. I have many perks, including provided housing and car allowance, gasoline. The list is long. Bottom line, after I finished putting Leilani through grad school, I have had no real expenses. I've invested. Luckily, despite my lack of financial skill, I've done superbly well." He leaned forward. "I bought Amazon stock long ago," he confided.

Mig leaned back in his chair. "I want to be your lender. No interest. Open-ended term."

Christel's hand flew to her chest. "Mig...Amazon stock?"

He grinned. "And Facebook."

Ava's daughter covered her mouth with her hand. For one of the first times ever, she was speechless.

Ava covered Mig's hand with her own. "Mig, you are family. More, you are my trusted friend. But I can't possibly..."

"Then make me a partner. In the golf course." He looked to Christel. "You could draft incorporation papers and that would be the sole asset. The golf course could make a hefty lease payment to Pali Maui each year. That's fair. You can't argue that."

He looked between them waiting for confirmation.

Christel still had her hand over her mouth. She slowly lowered it. "Amazon stock? Facebook?" She looked tentatively at her mother. "His proposal could work."

Mig placed both hands on the table and stood. "Then it's a deal." He didn't wait for Ava to confirm she'd go along with the plan. Instead, he turned to Christel. "Paper the deal," he directed with a wide grin.

He gave them both a hug. "This meeting is officially over. I've got work to do." He winked and headed for the door.

"Mig, wait!" Ava called out.

He turned.

"Thank you," she said, choking back emotion. Not over the extension of the much-needed funds, but that he would come to their rescue. "Now get back to work...partner," she added with a wink of her own.

16

Jon opened the passenger side door of Katie's blue SUV and climbed in beside his daughter. He buckled up and looked over at Willa. "You ready?"

She gripped the steering wheel and nodded. "Ready."

After weeks of hounding, Jon had finally given into Willa's pleas to learn to drive. Katie had, in no uncertain terms, made it clear the job fell to him, saying, "I did the whole *you're becoming a woman* talk. It's your turn now."

Jon cleared his throat. "Okay, your seat is adjusted, you're buckled in and you've adjusted your mirrors. The next thing is to start the engine." He'd given her a book to read and saw her pouring over it in her bedroom. He hoped she had at least absorbed 90 percent of the instruction contained within the pages.

She looked at him, let out a slightly nervous giggle, and did as she was told.

The engine roared to life.

"Okay, the plan is to back up and then put the car in drive and head for the road leading to the fields."

"Which?" she asked. "The upper or lower south?"

Jon pointed to a dirt roadway. "South." He gave her an encouraging smile. "Okay, you know what to do next?"

She nodded enthusiastically and put her mother's car in reverse. She glanced in the rearview mirror, then at her side mirror.

"Good job," he commended.

Willa smiled and carefully pressed the gas pedal. The car started moving. She pressed a little harder, too far and too fast, sending the vehicle jolting backward.

In an impulse, Willa slammed on the brakes, which sent both of them flying forward in their seats.

Looking impish, she swallowed. "Sorry."

Jon shook his head. "No, no that's how you learn...and why seatbelts are important. Try again."

His heart squeezed a little. His little girl was growing up. Jon couldn't help but wonder how this moment in time had arrived so fast? Seemed like only yesterday when they brought Willa home from the hospital and he held that tiny infant in his arms.

Mothers weren't the only ones who got up in the wee hours of the night when your sweet infant girl woke and cried...when you tried every single way you knew to soothe her and nothing seemed to work, and eventually the tears of joy you expected became tears of exhaustion and frustration.

It was one of those times when Jon lifted Willa to his chest and there, against the warmth of his bare skin, she settled down and finally slept. He remembered leaning in the darkness and kissing her soft downy head and regretfully thinking how she was too young to remember that moment.

He would never forget.

Jon often wondered if all the things he'd taught her, and all the conversations he'd had with her would be enough. He'd told her often that he expected her to always do her best. And her best was always good enough.

When she was out with friends, he hoped she would be a leader rather than a follower. Thankfully, the cyber bullying situation they had experienced had proven she had a good head on her shoulders.

"Dad?"

Her voice startled him, brought him back to the moment. Willa was leaning forward in her seat, her intense gaze directed out the windshield. Her knuckles were nearly white from gripping the steering wheel so tight as she directed the car carefully down the dirt road.

He gave her a smile. "Yeah?"

"Am I doing it right?"

He patted her leg. "You sure are, Baby. I'm proud of you."

Willa maneuvered a tight corner. Pleased with her accomplishment, she looked over at him. "I'm just glad Mom's not teaching me."

"Why's that, honey?"

"She's been so lame lately. I mean, really. Like I borrowed some of her piecing crème hair product without asking and she went ballistic."

"We all need to give Mom a little slack these days," he told her. "She's been going through a lot. Remember how it felt when you encountered that situation with those awful pics being sent around school? Well, you aren't the only one with stuff."

Willa scowled. "What stuff?"

"Private stuff. The point I'm making is that we need to consider we don't know what people are dealing with. Sometimes we just need to extend some grace, in spite of the way they are acting."

They drove past a row of sunflowers that had been planted along the outer field. While most of the crop is self-propagated by replanting crowns, bees and hummingbirds were key to cross-pollination.

"See those sunflowers, Willa?"

She nodded. "Yeah."

"Well, honey...it's like this. Did you know sunflowers turn according to the position of the sun? In other words, they 'chase the light.' While its rare here on Maui, what do you suppose happens on cloudy and rainy days when the sun is completely covered by clouds? Do you think the sunflower withers or turns its head toward the ground?"

He paused and told her to stop the car as he sought her full attention. "This is what happens. The sunflowers turn toward each other to share their energy. Nature's perfection is amazing and has so much to teach us. Likewise, Honey, we need to follow that example. Let's support one another and be the light during their cloudy times, especially when it comes to family."

He reached and chucked her chin. "Okay?"

Willa's face softened into a smile. "Yeah, I get it."

Jon swelled with satisfaction as her teenage angst faded a bit. "All right, sweetheart. Eyes back on the road. We have some driving to do."

17

"Wake up, sleepy head." Christel gradually pulled her eyes open out of a deep sleep to see Evan standing bedside with a breakfast tray in his hands. Her heart fluttered slightly at the sight of her new husband.

"I hope you're hungry," he said with a grin.

She sat up, rubbed the sleep from her eyes and ran her hands through her hair. "What is this?"

He positioned the tray over her lap. "It's eggs benedict and crispy bacon. With fresh-squeezed orange juice and a mug of steaming coffee—strong and black, the way you like it."

Touched by his gesture, she leaned for a closer look. "You did this?"

Evan made a big show of looking around. "You think I'm only good at fixating a knee cap?"

Suddenly, she was starving. She grabbed the fork, lifted the linen napkin and tucked it into the front of her nightgown. "No argument from me. You're a keeper."

That made him laugh. "I hope so." He held up his hand and displayed his wedding band. "You're stuck with me now."

"And happily so," she said. "Where's your breakfast?"

He patted his stomach. "I did a lot of taste testing." He sat on the edge of the bed and patted her leg. "Eat up."

Christel was happy to comply. She dug in, not bothering to refrain from talking with her mouth full. Funny, she'd only been married a short time but already she had a whole new comfort level with Evan. He was her husband...and that changed everything.

"So, I overheard you talking on the phone to your mom," he mentioned. "Mig is financially partnering on the golf course renovation?"

She scooped a bite of poached egg covered in hollandaise onto her fork. "You heard correctly. I admit that initially, I was a bit reluctant to accept his generous offer. It's my practice to never hire anyone you can't fire and to never lend money, or accept money, from family or close friends. Then it hit me that I was being silly. Agreeing to Mig's offer is no different than accepting a loan from strangers. Besides, I've known Mig for years. He's worked for Pali Maui ever since I can even remember."

She sipped her coffee. "When we were little, Katie and I played with his daughter, Leilani. We loved to build forts using the shipping pallets. Katie always called the rickety structures playhouses, but they were definitely forts."

Evan laughed. "Why, pray tell, did you little girls have to have a fortress? What enemies were you warding off here on Pali Maui?"

Christel grew wide-eyed and shoved the last of the bacon in her mouth. "The pineapple monsters, of course."

They both laughed.

"It was Leilani who came up with the idea of creating life-sized dolls out of stray boards. Under her very exact directions, we nailed shipping twine to the top of the board as hair and then painted on the features...the noses, eyes and mouths. We even dressed the board dolls using material from leftover curtains Mom was going to toss." Christel smiled at the fond memory. "My doll was named Easter."

Evan cocked his head. "Easter? That's an odd name for a doll."

"Yet entirely appropriate for someone who had been resurrected from the board pile."

"So, where is Mig's daughter now?" he asked.

"She lives in Seattle. Last I heard, Mig said her highly-successful PR firm recently landed a contract with a big-selling romance author." She dabbed the napkin at her mouth. "Apparently, romance authors make buckets of money."

Evan grinned and patted her leg again. "Well, I could sit here all day reminiscing with my beautiful bride. Unfortunately, I've got a surgery scheduled for this morning, a hip replacement." He leaned and kissed her cheek. "See you tonight?"

Her hand cupped his cheek with affection. "The pressure is on to reciprocate. I'm an abysmal cook, so I'll have to think of something else."

"It's not a gift if you think you have to respond with a corresponding gesture." A sly smile formed on that handsome face of his. "Of course, any and all bedtime favors are always appreciated. And I'm a sucker for back rubs."

Finished, she handed him the breakfast tray. "So noted."

TRY AS SHE MIGHT, Ava could not get over how Mig came to their rescue with his generous offer to supply their much-needed financing for the golf renovation. She didn't want to admit it, even to herself, but had they not secured financing they would have suffered consequences, including losing Tom Strobe and all the other contractors lined up.

Mig had saved the day with his offer.

It was a well-established fact that Pali Maui would be hard pressed to run as efficiently, or successfully, if Miguel Nakamoa was not at the helm of all the operations. Over the years, his contribution to the success of Pali Maui had been immeasurable. Certainly, her father had thought so before his passing.

Yes, Mig had been an incredible help, not only carrying out his regular duties, but taking on any task as necessary, especially since she had lost Lincoln. Not that her deceased husband was involved in Pali Maui's operation. He was much more focused on the publicity side of things...which was another way of saying he left the hard work to others while he climbed on the stage and took all the credit.

Mig was exactly the opposite. He worked behind the scenes, never needing accolades. He was not only her trusted employee, but a friend and confidant. Now he was her partner financially.

Ava hoped Mig would never be sorry he extended the loan and that the partnership would be financially lucrative for all the parties. According to Christel's projections, the renovation had the potential to increase revenue substantially.

Because Mig saved the day, they were thankfully able to keep their agreement with Tom Strobe. In fact, she was meeting him in a few minutes to hammer out the final start date.

No sooner had this thought crossed her mind and Tom's car pulled up to the offices. A smile formed and Ava quickly headed out to meet him. "Tom! So good to see you again."

He smiled back. "I was looking forward to it. I have so many ideas." He opened the back seat of his car and pulled out rolls of schematics.

Ava motioned for the office. "Well, come on inside and let's get started."

Over the course of the next several hours, she and Tom poured over the drawings and plans, carefully detailing all his diagrams and plans. There was a reason Tom Strobe was so well respected in the golf community. His ideas were exceptionally fresh and innovative.

For example, he designed the new course to work its way up to a much higher elevation than currently existed which would provide even greater commanding views of the ocean in the distance, with the following holes descending back to the clubhouse in a pronounced fashion that looped through cleverly placed water hazards. He also included a par four on the sixth hole that featured a dramatic drop shot to a half-hidden but wide landing area surrounded by rolling terrain framed by dense trees, ferns, and tropical plants. There were also some impressive doglegs and elevation changes, building to an entertaining climax on what would inevitably be one of Hawaii's most demanding closing holes.

When she praised his ideas, he simply replied, "The quality of a golf hole is not based on length, but how interesting it is to play."

She learned technological advancements in golf equipment had changed the way the game of golf was played. Every year, club and ball manufacturers introduced new models with the promise of more distance and better ball flight control. As a result, golfers of all playing levels and experience were consistently hitting the ball farther.

Tom pointed to his plans. "The key is to fashion fairway, roughs, bunkering, trees, and mounding, all with unexpected features."

Ava's stomach grumbled rather loudly, reminding her they had worked well past lunchtime. "I love everything about your plans, Tom. I couldn't have hoped for any better. I hope you'll let me show my gratitude by joining me for lunch."

He glanced at his watch. "Oh, my goodness. I completely got caught up in talking over these plans. You must be hungry."

She admitted that she was indeed ready for some food.

"Will you join me? We can go catch a bite over at No Ka 'Oi. Jon said earlier that he was getting in a shipment of fresh calamari."

"Excellent. I've been dreaming of eating there again ever since you introduced me to your son-in-law's talents."

Over lunch, Ava learned renovation like what they had planned could take up to a year to complete. Tom estimated theirs would be finished in about nine months, give or take, and depending on the weather.

"Thankfully, Maui enjoys many sunny days," he told her.

Ava caught herself once again entertaining the notion that having Tom around for a while was a good thing.

"I have to say, Ava, I'm duly impressed with everything you have built here at Pali Maui. I especially admire the family aspect and how all of your children, whether they are officially employed here, all contribute."

She traced the stem of the wine glass with her finger. "Family definitely has it's challenges. Even so, my children are the most important thing to me."

He smiled across the table. "It shows. Your kids are amazing human beings. I'm jealous."

Ava couldn't help but wonder what kind of woman would leave a marriage after only two years. She was sad for Tom, that he had not been given the gift of a family.

Her lunchmate dabbed his mouth with his napkin and laid it on the table. "Tell you what, we've worked hard today. You up for a little break?"

She grinned. "What did you have in mind?"

"I had planned to go snorkeling this afternoon. I'd love it if you'd join me."

Ava mentally ran through the items left on her task list for the day. There was nothing that couldn't be postponed. She gave him an enthusiastic nod. "Sounds like a fantastic plan."

Less than an hour later, she and Tom were standing with

their snorkel gear on the coastline near the Coral Gardens, ready to climb on board Tom's inflatable motorized raft.

Coral Gardens offered a unique, beautiful natural reef formation in a protected bay, on the west side of Maui. The spot was home to many Hawaiian green sea turtles, and hundreds of species of fish. The location, which could only be accessed by boat, was known to be elite and private, with visibility reaching forty feet. Its crystal-clear waters and large coral heads made the underwater views for snorkeling breathtaking.

Minutes later, Tom anchored. He turned to Ava. "Ready?"

She nodded and secured her gear. She climbed up on the edge of the inflated raft and slid into the tepid water. Tom checked his anchor again and then followed her into the water.

In all the years Ava had lived in Maui, she'd had numerous occasions to go snorkeling—too many to count, actually. Regardless, every time she placed her face under the water's surface and viewed the panorama beneath, the sight nearly took her breath away.

Hundreds of thousands of years ago, lava from the Mauna Kahalawai crater flowed down into the ocean at this location, creating lava fingers that were now home to some of the most stunning tropical fish on the island...a certain feast for the eyes.

Ava let her gaze drift over at Tom. He pointed to a crevice about five feet below them pointing out a large school of lauhau, more commonly known as threadpin butterfly fish with their soft blue and bright yellow coloring and unique black dot.

Ava gave him a thumbs up and motioned to her left where bright red lolo fish darted back and forth.

Ava surfaced and blew residual water from her bore tube. She then returned her face to the water and let the motion of her fins take her back to Tom's side.

Suddenly, she looked over and, not far in the distance, one of the largest sea turtles she'd seen in some time drifted in front of them. From this close, she could see the hooded eye and trace the white outlines on its shell. Unafraid, the turtle moved even closer and looked directly at them as if to say hello.

Tom reached and grabbed her hand and squeezed.

His touch was as unexpected as the turtle, and sent her heart racing.

This.

This is what she missed so very much. The companionship of a man, a mate, a partner. Of course, she and Tom had barely known each other and were simply friends. Even so, she had to admit the feel of his calloused hand against her own sparked an intense yearning.

Ava was caught entirely off guard by this longing...a feeling that, frankly, terrified her.

18

"Oh, honey...you're a widow. You're not dead!" Alani scooped Ava's shoulders into the protection of her abundant arm and squeezed. "You are a healthy, normal woman. Of course, you're going to get a little twitterpated by a handsome man."

"This is not a Disney movie," Ava moaned. "And I'm not some princess who needs rescued out of a life void of relationship. I was married for years. Now, I have my children and grandchildren. I'm past all that. Besides, hot romances are for the young."

"You're not old!" Alani carried a bowl of rice over to the counter. "Besides, I think it's a good sign, a healthy sign. There will come a time when you'll want to move on after losing Lincoln. Perhaps sooner than later." She winked, then pointed to a large spoon on the counter that was just out of her reach. "Hand me that, will you?"

Ava stood next to her friend in the large commercial kitchen and reached for the spoon. How many times had she joined Alani while she prepared for the evening's luau? Each time, she laid her heart bare—the good, the bad, and the ugly. They had shared a lot, the two of them.

Their mutual pain over Lincoln and Mia's illicit relationship was an example. Few friends would have survived that kind of revelation. The kind of trust required for that type of open and vulnerable interaction was a treasure Ava cherished. She had suffered many losses over her years, but the loss of her best friend was something she wouldn't be able to bear.

Ava handed Alani the spoon, then spontaneously pulled her friend into a tight hug. "In case I don't tell you often enough...I love you, my friend."

"Ah, honey. The feeling is mutual." Alani hugged back, holding onto the spoon and squeezing.

Suddenly, Alani winced. She pulled away and her hand went to her breast.

Ava scowled. "Alani, what's the matter?"

Alani reached for the bowl of rice. "It's nothing."

Ignoring all propriety, Ava placed her hand against Alani's ample breast and pressed. Her eyes flew open. "Alani! You have a lump!"

"That? Oh, that's been there forever."

"How long is forever?" Ava demanded as she tried to determine the lump's size.

"Okay, I know it's been a while, but you don't need to feel up your best friend."

Ava scowled. "This isn't funny, Alani. You have a lump in your breast. You need to have that seen." She immediately pulled her phone from her pocket. "I'm calling Christel. Evan will know who the best cancer doctor..."

Alani lifted the phone from Ava's hand. "This isn't cancer. My mother had a similar lump in her breast and another in her leg. The lumps were there for years. It's fatty tissue. In case you haven't noticed, I'm a fat woman." She waved off the concern and poured a cup of soy sauce into the rice. "I swear, Ava. You do love drama."

"I do not love drama," Ava argued. "You are foolish not to have this checked. If it's not cancer, then you have nothing to worry about. If it is...well, do I need to remind you that breast cancer patients often survive? But, only if the cancer is caught early."

Alani rolled her eyes. "For goodness sakes, you are too much."

"I'm not taking no for an answer," Ava told her. "So don't even try to argue me out of this. I'm making you an appointment."

THAT EVENING, Evan returned home bringing another surprise. "Christel, what do you think about selling this place and buying a house together? I mean, I have my house and you have this one. We could put both on the market and get something bigger, a little more grand."

Christel stood at the kitchen sink, turned and looked at him like he'd grown two heads. "We are both busy professionals and never home. Why would we need a bigger place?"

A tiny smile nipped at the corners of his mouth. "For the family we're going to have?"

Shocked, Christel shut off the faucet and dried her hands. "Family? We haven't really talked about that." Of course, they hadn't talked about any of those things. He'd surprised her and they'd impulsively jumped into marriage. Not that she regretted her decision, not even a little. And yes, she did want children. It's just something they would need to plan for. Someday.

She explained that to Evan.

His response was simple, "Babe, I know I'm springing this

on you. There's no reason to wait, really. I'd like to start sooner, than later."

Christel's heart pounded. "Oh."

He cocked his head. "Want to expound on that a little? Is that something you would like to think about also?" He watched her with an anxious expression.

"Well, yes...I just don't know about the timing. Right now, I'm in the middle of the golf course renovation. I had no idea the hoops a company has to jump through from an ecological standpoint. Every modification to the layout, the soil structure, the foliage and trees...it all has to be preapproved by Maui Environmental Management. The paperwork alone has me buried."

Evan came around the island and took her damp hands in his. "There will never be a perfect time. My surgeries, my full-time practice, the medical boards I sit on....and your full plate —well, I simply doubt any of that will ever change. At least not significantly. And I don't want it to. I love our busy lives. I love that we both enjoy our professional lives and that others benefit from our work. But, honey...I really hope you'll consider what I'm saying."

Christel thought a moment. She'd always wanted a family. In fact, as Jay's addiction grew, the air in her mommy balloon had deflated. She'd simply been forced into the realization that getting pregnant was completely off the table. Then came the divorce.

While Evan didn't say so, neither of them were getting any younger.

Christel looked him directly in the eyes. "How many children do you want?" Funny, how she wore his wedding ring and yet they'd never even discussed future plans for a family.

"I'm open," he conceded. "At least two? Maybe three?"

She nodded. "Yes, we can't possibly rob our child of siblings." Another realization hit. If they were to have three children, she would indeed have to start soon. Lots of women have babies after forty these days, but it was still safer for both mother and child if the pregnancy happened earlier, which meant she didn't have a lot of time.

Christel nervously squeezed her husband's hands. "Okay, you certainly are good at springing things on a girl. I, too, want a family and can see the wisdom in giving the idea some serious consideration. It's just that the idea is coming at me a little too fast. I'd like some time to enjoy my new husband before letting my body blow up into pregnancy." She pulled her hands from his and smiled. "Do me a favor? Just give me a week or two to let the idea settle a bit. Maybe longer."

Evan laughed. "Of course. Whatever time you need, you've got." His eyes grew intense. "Until then, perhaps we need to practice." He took hold of her hand and led her to the bedroom.

19

Shane rubbed his weary eyes as he wandered the grocery store aisles plucking items from the shelves and tossing them into the cart while Carson slept soundly in the sling tied tightly across Shane's chest.

Shane shook his head. No wonder the baby was out like a light. He hadn't slept at all last night. Neither had Shane.

The night had been a long one. Carson was starting to teethe and nothing Shane did seemed to comfort the little guy. Finally, he gave up and called his mother at about midnight to ask for advice.

"Mom, what do I do? Carson is screaming from the top of his lungs. Obviously, he's hurting."

"Did you try a cold washcloth?"

"Yeah. I read that on the internet. But he's still crying."

"Did you use pressure? Often pushing down on the gums a little, not too hard, will relieve the ache."

Carson's bellows grew even more loud. "I don't know, Mom. I just can't seem to do anything that helps."

She must've heard the desperation in his voice. "Do you want me to come?"

"Nah, that's a long way."

"I'll be there soon." She hung up before he could protest further.

Less than an hour later, he heard a light knock on the door. He opened it to find his mom standing there looking beautiful, even at this time of night. He'd always admired her. She was smart, worked hard, loved her family, and was one of the prettiest moms he knew. Really, she like had it going on. How his dad could cheat on her, he'd never get.

Shane drew Ava into a hug. "He's still crying."

Ava joined him inside. "I can hear that."

She lifted a tiny bottle out of her jacket pocket. "I brought a bottle of clove oil."

Shane scowled. "Clove oil?"

"It works. At least it did on all four of you kids."

Shane followed her into the nursery and watched as his mom lifted his baby boy from the crib and patted him on the back. She carried her grandson to the rocking chair and sat.

"Honey, could you take the lid off?" She lifted the bottle to Shane.

He removed the cap and passed the tiny brown bottle back into her hands and watched as she covered the opening with the pad of her forefinger, tipped the bottle upside down. She lifted the clove oil, returning it to him and he took it.

"Here, sweet boy," she cooed, as she rubbed her grandson's gums with the oil. "This will make it all better."

Almost immediately, Carson stopped crying. He sniffled and nestled his tiny head against his grandmother's shoulder and almost immediately closed his eyes. He gave a last whiffle and drew a deep breath, and nodded off to sleep.

"Wow," Shane said. "That worked."

Ava smiled and stood. She laid Carson back in his bed and turned, motioning for Shane to follow her.

In the living room, he offered her something to drink. "I

know it's late. Do you want to catch a wink here, Mom?" He pointed down the hall. "I don't have much furniture yet so the guest room is pretty bare. But you can take my bed. I'll sleep out here on the sofa."

Ava took Shane's chin in her hand. "Thanks, sweetheart. But no, I'll head home. I have an early morning appointment…" Her words drifted off and a tear sprouted.

"Mom? What is it? What's the matter?" He took her by the shoulders. "You're upset."

Ava sighed and nodded. She confided what she'd learned about Alani, and how concerned she was over the discovery.

"Ah, Mom. Maybe you shouldn't jump to the worst-case scenario. I mean, you don't know it's cancer. Right?"

Ava nodded miserably. "I called Christel and Evan arranged to have her biopsied in the morning over at the hospital." She glanced at her watch. "Well, this morning."

Shane placed a hand on her forearm. "Don't borrow trouble. Let's wait and see what the test reveals."

His mom gave him a weak smile and nodded. "Yeah, I suppose you're right. We'll know soon."

Shane drew his mom into a hug. "Everything is going to be okay, Mom. You'll see."

AVA MET ORI, Elta, and Alani at Maui Memorial at the scheduled time and together they took the elevator up to radiology. First, a mammogram would show the parameters of the mass. This would be followed by an ultrasound-guided biopsy that would require a small incision about a quarter of an inch long under local anesthetic.

Ori, Elta, and Ava waited in the small area outside radiology after they took Alani back for the procedure. While waiting,

Ava flipped through an old magazine filled with Halloween decorating tips.

"How long do you think it will take?" Ori asked. While his voice was steady, Ava could tell her friend's son was fighting a case of the nerves.

"Evan told me the procedure would only take fifteen to thirty minutes," she told him. She smiled with as much confidence as she could muster. Alani would want her to remain calm and help Alani's family. If she let her emotions have full rein, she'd fall apart. That would do none of them any good.

She stared at a glossy page filled with images of porches decorated with pumpkins and mums.

Despite her determination, her insides quivered. Typically, Ava was steady-natured. The idea of her best friend being ill—perhaps more—well, it shook her to the core.

Alani was often the one to get riled over things. Yet, she had seemed so calm when the doctor wanted to see her immediately. "It's nothing," she claimed, yet again, as if by repeating the notion it would be true.

Evan entered the waiting area and smiled over at her. "Any news?"

Ava shook her head. "Not yet. They just took her back." It was then that she noticed Christel standing behind him.

"I'm here for moral support," she reported.

"We both are," Evan said, taking a seat across from them.

Elta thanked them for being there. "How long do these things take?" he asked, apparently forgetting that she'd already mentioned it would only take about twenty minutes or so.

Evan leaned his elbows on his legs. "The procedure won't take long. We won't have results right away. Normally, the lab can take up to two to three days to report back. I've asked for a professional favor. They will be expediting Alani's tissue samples."

Elta's face filled with gratitude. "I can't thank you enough, Doctor...I mean, Evan."

As predicted, the radiologist appeared a short while later. Upon seeing Evan, she waved him over. "Can I speak with you a moment?" She motioned to a corner of the room.

Ava felt ready to explode. That was certainly not a good sign...was it?

Seconds later, Evan returned. "I'm afraid the radiologist thinks it's a good idea to go a step further today. There seems to be secondary lumps deeper in the breast tissue."

The radiologist quickly provided further explanation. "Sometimes the deeper we go, the more painful. It's better if we put Alani under a general anesthesia...but only for a very short time," she quickly added. "We want to get really good specimens."

Elta looked scared. He nodded. "Of course, do whatever is necessary."

Christel's arm went around Ava as they took their seats again. "Mom, don't borrow trouble."

She nodded absently. Why does everyone keep telling her that? Do they even realize what it would do to her to lose Alani? She'd become a widow only a year before. It was Alani who journeyed that with her, right by her side. Her best friend had a knack for knowing when to simply remain quiet. "Be still, and know God," was her often repeated statement, a favorite Bible verse.

Ava attempted to calm herself and mentally repeated that now. She couldn't. Her mind was like a whale breeching the surface of the water then crashing back into the ocean sending spraying waves in all directions. All the what-ifs haunted her until she could barely breathe.

Surprisingly, anger flooded. Why in the world had Alani brushed something like this off? Why had she waited so long to let anyone know about the lump? If today brought news they hoped would not be delivered, the delay would be the culprit. She wanted to take Alani and shake her by those thick shoulders. Cancer was nothing to fool with. Ava's own mother had died when she was a child. She knew what a ferocious animal cancer could be...how it snuck up on you and attacked, biting until the victim was left lifeless.

Tears sprouted and she quickly wiped them away before anyone could notice.

Evan saw.

He stood and came over. "I know what you are thinking, Ava." He knelt in front of her. "Let me warn again, we do not know what we're dealing with. There are plenty of other possibilities beyond the worst."

Elta nodded. "Her mother had fat cysts."

Evan gave him an encouraging look. "Yes, like I said, we don't know what this is until the tests tell us. That said, if the biopsy reveals anything concerning, I have plenty of connections. This is not a battle she will fight alone."

His hand covered Ava's. "And neither will you."

20

Vanessa typed out another text to her sister. The third that morning. All had gone unanswered.

She loved her sibling, but they hadn't always been close. It was for this very reason that there remained distance, even after a perfunctory reconciliation earlier this year.

After being fired from the news station, Vanessa had packed up what little material possessions she actually owned and made the bold move to show up on Ava's doorstep, unannounced. She'd feared what her sister's reaction might be. Worse...that she would be turned away. They had been estranged for years. Ava flat out didn't like her. The way Vanessa saw the situation, that was just fine by her. She didn't need some judgmental broad heckling over all her decisions, claiming she constantly fell short of showing any sort of wisdom whatsoever. Heavens, she had an ex-husband who filled that role just fine, thank you.

Surprisingly, while her initial reception had been a little chilly, Ava finally warmed up. In the end, her sister took pity on her despairing financial state and offered her a place to live.

Nothing fancy. Just one of the worker shanties. But it was a place and it was free. And it was appreciated.

The best thing about being forced to relocate was reconnecting with her nieces and nephews. Thanks to her ex pushing the narrative that she had put her career before family, she was estranged from her own daughter. It felt good to reconnect with family.

She glanced at the sea-turtle-shaped tattoo on her inner forearm, the one she'd gotten along with her nephew, Shane. She was especially close to that one. Seemed they both were free spirits and had a lot in common.

He, too, had been dealt a very unexpected blow by life. Like her, he'd accepted what couldn't be changed. He'd picked himself up and dusted off, embracing fatherhood and all that went with it.

As for her, she had done much the same. Termination from the news anchor position she adored could have crumpled her, left her unable to muster up enough self-confidence to move forward. That wasn't her style. Even so, she'd mentally suffered and had to fight and tell herself not to listen to those voices in her head that wanted to take her down.

Vanessa let a smile form as she tucked the phone away and looked around the campaign office.

No one who chose to languish in their junk ever got ahead. Her about-face, her determination...well, it had paid off. Just look at her now. She was the Media and Communications director for a campaign that would, no doubt, send Jim Kahele to Washington, DC.

Satisfied with herself, she headed for her glass cubicle.

Twenty minutes later, Jim stuck his head inside. "You up for lunch?"

"Yes! I'm starving." She grabbed her purse.

They went to one of her favorite lunch spots, Star Noodle. Located on the waterfront, with ocean views to die for, the

Asian-inspired restaurant was one of Maui's destination eateries where locals and tourists flocked for reservations.

Jim didn't need a reservation. There were some people who moved through open doors where ever they went. Her boss was one of those.

Admittedly, Vanessa enjoyed being seen with the future state senator from Hawaii. From what she could tell, he enjoyed being seen with her as well. The key was to fan his attraction without letting it flame up and burn them both professionally.

He placed his hand on the small of her back and guided her to a table underneath the outdoor pergola. At night, the strings of lights would illumine pots of bamboo and tropical foliage positioned among the tables. Of course, the lights were not needed in the middle of the day.

Jim ordered Nuoc Cham Chicken, a delicious-looking dish of boneless chicken breast cooked in a savory sauce with peanuts, mint and cilantro over the top. She selected eggplant in miso with sesame seeds and fried garlic. The garlic would require mints after eating, but would be worth it.

When their waitress finished taking their orders and retreated from the table, Jim turned to her. "So, how do you think we're doing...really?"

Vanessa's face brightened. "The polls are coming back with strong indicators that you are the favored candidate. I've learned to trust my gut, and my gut is telling me you are building trust with the voters. Our messaging is strong and your positions well taken." She grinned. "I think I'm looking at our new state senator."

Jim drew a deep breath. "I hope you're correct. I'm hearing from some principal players in our party that our opponent is edging up on the environmental issues." He reached for her hand.

She shook her head and slowly pulled her hand back. "Not a good idea. Especially in public," she reminded. She did not remind him that a personal relationship, especially one of a romantic nature, was behind them. The campaign could not risk any scandal. Worse, she could not risk being bored out of her mind. While Jim's political aspirations were exciting, his strategies in the bedroom made her yawn.

"About the environmental issues, I hear Pali Maui is putting in a golf course?"

"Extended the existing course," Vanessa clarified. "From what I understand, my sister is working with Tom Strobe, one of the top designers around."

"About that...I hope nothing associated with your family could raise issues. Environmentally speaking."

Vanessa straightened. *Quit skirting the issue,* she thought. She hated when people failed to be direct and speak their mind. She certainly intended to do just that.

"Look, Jim. Ava has performed all the prerequisites and jumped through all the hoops. The Environmental Impact Statement was returned with a favorable finding. That simply is not an issue."

He looked skeptical. "Perhaps not. But we both know reality and perception can be two very different things. While the impact may be within acceptable boundaries, one hint otherwise might hurt the campaign."

Vanessa threw her head back and laughed. "You worry far too much. I create the messaging and when I'm through with my effort, voters will beg to hold your victory party in the Pali Maui clubhouse!"

21

"Cancer?" Ava's voice cracked as she repeated the diagnosis.

Evan looked across his desk to where Ava, Christel, Elta, and Alani sat. Normally, news of this sort would be provided directly to the patient in line with medical privacy rules. Alani had insisted on having her "team" with her, firmly stating, "So you can all see how silly you're being when we find the lump is just what I said...fatty tissue."

The solemn look on her son-in-law's face said far more than the treacherous words out of his mouth. "Are you sure?" Ava asked. "It's cancer?"

He nodded, stood and sat on the corner of his desk. Evan looked uncomfortable, but looked Alani directly in the eye. "The results from the tests I ordered were not as we'd hoped. Like I said, there is a finding of cancerous cells. It will take additional time to actually type the tissue and know exactly what kind of cancer, but we won't wait. I've contacted a professional friend who practices in Honolulu, Dr. Barry Hinske. He's one of the best oncologists I know. He agreed to see you immediately, as a professional courtesy."

Elta looked entirely wrecked. "*Kāhāhāi ka 'ino,*" he murmured. "What does that mean?"

"It means the lump needs to come out." Evan took a deep breath. "Depending on what Dr. Hinske finds during the lumpectomy, it is possible he may recommend a full mastectomy. In cases like these, it is better to be aggressive and reduce risk."

Christel bobbed her head in agreement. "Yes, there is no reason not to get out ahead of this."

Ava sat there, stunned. She wanted to say something helpful, something encouraging and comforting. No words came.

Instead, tears burned at her eyes. All she could do is reach and grab her dear friend's hand and squeeze. At the same time, a prayer formed inside her head.

Please, Lord. Protect my friend.

Evan noticed Ava's emotion and assured everyone, "This is not a death sentence. Many strides have been made in the oncology field, especially when it comes to breast cancers. There is no evidence to support the theory that rapidly growing cancers are more prone to metastasize."

"Metastasize?" Elta choked out.

Christel turned. "That means spreading to other parts of the body."

Alani stood and held out open palms. "Okay, everybody out. I need to talk to Evan...alone." She challenged their surprised looks. "I mean it. Out!" She turned to her beloved husband. "Even you, Elta."

Reluctantly, they all rose and paraded out of Evan's office. No one spoke as they leaned against the hallway walls and waited.

Minutes later, the door to Evan's office opened and Alani appeared. She hoisted her purse up on her arm. "Okay, drop the sad faces. Not one minute of my existence comes as a surprise to God...not even this. I don't need all of you planning my funeral already."

She looked Ava directly in the eye and pointed. "And that, most assuredly, means you."

AVA FELT like she'd been hit in the stomach with a brick. She sat in the passenger seat as Christel drove her home. Thankfully, her daughter had the good sense to remain quiet. Ava needed time to let this information saturate her being. She needed to think.

Evan was right. Women fought breast cancer and often won these days. A positive finding wasn't the death sentence it used to be. Sure, Alani was facing surgery, perhaps major surgery. After that she'd have radiation and maybe even chemotherapy. No doubt, this was going to be a war.

Of all of the people dearest to her, Alani was known to be the warrior. She would take this fight on with all weapons drawn. Ava would most certainly hear her dear friend say repeatedly, "Our battle is against the evil one and his wicked ways, and all the lies he whispers. That serpent of old would like to fill us with fear. Remember...only God gives life and only God takes it away. I am in His hands. Let's not forget that."

Ava couldn't help herself. She smiled. Her friend was a pastor's wife, through and through. She loved the Lord, and it showed.

Ava could only wish her faith was as strong.

Her phone rang then. Ava pulled it from the bottom of her purse and answered.

"Ava, it's Alani. Put me on speaker, would you please?"

Ava did as she was instructed.

"Listen you two," Alani said through the phone speaker. "I

think I need to warn you of something. I've called Mia and I asked her to come home. Elta is picking her up at the airport tomorrow. I thought you both should know."

22

The minute Christel got home she pulled her phone out and texted her brothers and sister. *"I need to talk to all of you right away. Privately. Meet me in the parking lot at Waihe'e Ridge Trail in an hour."*

Katie was the first to reply. *"Okay, drama queen. What's up?"*

The boys chimed in as well. Shane complained he had Carson and needed to feed him dinner. Aiden said he badly needed a shower after a day cleaning the rescue truck out.

Christel sighed and quickly tapped out, *"We're all busy. This is important. Just be there."*

Aiden had already arrived when Christel pulled into the parking lot. He leaned against his Jeep sipping from a Starbucks cup. He waved upon seeing her.

Before Christel could get out of her car, both Katie and Shane pulled in.

Christel shielded her eyes from the setting sun that cast a hint of mango-colored hue across the far horizon as she watched a surfer mount his board to the top of his car.

"What's up?" Shane hollered as he unbuckled and pulled Carson from his car seat. "I need to make this quick. Little dude will throw a fit soon if he doesn't get his mashed bananas."

Christel held up open hands. "Look, I wouldn't yell 'Fire!' unless we were all about to get burned."

Katie's brows drew together. "Okay, okay. Spill already."

Christel quickly explained about Alani's test findings. Before her brothers and sister could respond, she immediately added, "But Alani's cancer finding is not what this is about."

Aiden drew his hand across the top of his hair. "What *is* this little meeting about?"

"Mia is returning to the island."

Her statement landed with every bit of the heaviness she knew it would.

Katie shook her head. "Why?"

Aiden rolled his eyes. "Don't be dumb. Of course, she'd come home to be with her mom at a time like this. I mean, think about it."

Shane held out his finger and Carson wrapped his tiny hand tightly around it and smiled. "Well, we knew this day would be here eventually. It doesn't mean we're forced to have anything to do with her."

"Oh, yeah?" Christel challenged. "How are we going to be there for Mom and support her through her best friend's cancer journey without eventually running into Alani's daughter? Like perhaps in a hospital waiting room? I know, we can just make appointments and take turns supporting our mothers. Yes, I'm sure Mia would agree to be so kind. Or, maybe I should call that traitor by a more appropriate name, like—"

"Not helpful," Aiden interrupted. He tossed his empty coffee container into a nearby trash receptacle. "Look, Christel. I'm glad you gave us a heads-up, but the reality is just as Shane said. As much as we all dreaded it, we all knew this day would come."

Katie parked her hands on her hips. "This isn't about us,

guys. This is about Mom. Facing Mia is only going to bring up all the hurts from the past. It's scarcely been a year since Mom's heart was crushed...first by the knowledge Dad died in a car accident, and then by learning he had an affair with her best friend's daughter. The girl we grew up with and thought was our friend."

"Yeah," Shane admitted. "Mia Kané redefined the term friend."

Carson fussed a little and Christel lifted him from her brother's arms, jiggling him back and forth to calm him. "Well, I say we need a united front. What is our position going to be?"

Katie straightened and lifted her chin. "Our position is that Mia is a...well, I'm not saying it out loud. We need to do everything in our power to protect Mom."

Christel quickly chimed in. "Agreed!"

Aiden rubbed the back of his neck. "There goes that joy Mom and Uncle Jack tried to drive down our throats."

"We have joy," Katie argued. "Lots of joy! As long as Mia stays as far away from this family as possible."

23

The alarm went off but Ava was already awake. She carried a steaming mug of coffee with her as she headed for her bathroom to prepare for the day.

Only weeks after breaking ground on the golf course renovation, marked strides had been made in the project. It had taken effort, but permits had all been obtained, including the elusive environmental permissions. With licensing in hand, the real work began.

Back hoes arrived, as did a team of excavation workers, landscapers, and water drainage specialists. While enjoying bright and sunny days most of the year, the Maui skies had been known to burst with rainstorms that could create torrential streams of rushing water popping up out of nowhere. It was critical that the topography be designed to avert any damage from those sudden storms.

Thankfully, Tom was in control and that gave Ava confidence all was done properly, relieving her of the need to think about any issues that could arise.

Ava jumped in the shower, having a difficult time concentrating on anything these days, let alone juggling the demands of running Pali Maui with a massive golf renovation. For the past few days, her thoughts were fully captured with Alani's cancer. And, if she dared to admit it, she dreaded Mia's return to the island.

Out of sight, out of mind.

Ava had heard the popular adage hundreds of times. In some ways, she'd proved the saying true. As long as Mia was gone, Ava didn't have to dwell on the betrayal she'd suffered at the hands of her husband and best friend's daughter. She didn't have to picture them in that house together, laughing and holding hands as they drove the winding Road to Hana while returning home from their secret trysts.

No one knew how long she'd been haunted with the images she'd encountered inside the house Lincoln had secretly purchased...the fashion magazines on the coffee table in the living room, the toiletries and woman's slippers in the bathroom, the pretty pillow cases...or that dreadful plaque mounted above the bed Lincoln and Mia had slept in. The plaque that mimicked an old Hawaiian saying.

Ua ola loko I ke aloha - Love gives life within.

The stricken look on Alani's face that day when they'd made the trip to Hana had said so much.

Ava learned later that the phrase had been often repeated by Alani's mother and that the plaque had been a gift from Alani's mother to her daughter, Mia.

She'd worked to scrub her mind of all those horrid memories in order to embrace joy and purpose that extended well past that betrayal.

Now, all that was about to be threatened.

Despite Ava's steadfast decision to move on...sadly, the mention of Mia's name and the notion she was returning to the island brought every hurt rushing back.

Ava shut off the water in the shower and stepped out. She toweled off, dressed and applied a little makeup, then headed out to meet with Tom Strobe.

"There you are," he said upon seeing her. He beamed as he made a sweeping motion with his arm, inviting her to see the progress so far. "Well, what do you think?"

"I think you are amazing. I'm thrilled with the headway you've made."

In the distance, a bulldozer pushed a mound of dark, rich dirt into a pile. A front loader then scooped up the earth and transported it away from the area that Tom's rolled-up plans indicated would soon become a water hazard.

Tom frowned. "Ava? Are you okay? You look troubled."

She sighed. "I didn't sleep very well last night."

"Something bothering you? Don't feel pressured to share, but my ear is all yours. I'm a good listener." He gave her an encouraging smile.

Ava glanced his way wishing she was better at hiding her feelings. Her issues were private. She thought it best to keep it that way.

As if sensing her reluctance, Tom pushed his aviator sunglasses up into his brown hair speckled with gray. He gave her another smile and when he did, the sides of his eyes crinkled.

He was good looking. Not in a flashy sort of way. More down to earth. Certainly nothing like Lincoln with his designer blazers, crisply pressed button-downs, and loafers.

She mentally rolled her eyes. Even in the field, her former husband dressed like he was going to the Met...and she didn't mean the baseball game. Despite hating art, he still used related terms and phrases he'd read on the internet just to impress people.

He impressed someone, all right...Mia.

Ava pointed. "What's that?" she asked, trying to divert her own thoughts.

Tom nodded in that direction. "That? It's a grader. You'll be seeing a lot of those around here as we sculpt the new fairways and fashion the greens."

He looked her way. "By the way, I heard a rumor that *Golf Digest* magazine is interested in doing a story on the renovation. Some folks I know on staff gave me a heads-up via an email."

Ava reacted with enthusiasm. "That's terrific. Great exposure. Hopefully, this renovation will show return on the investment in short order. A lot is riding on this project." Especially now that her good friend and trusted operations manager had risked his own finances. She didn't want to let Mig down.

"I'm sure you're going to be pleasantly surprised at the destination golfers who will show up to check out the latest course. Especially when they hear about the sixth hole."

Tom had made it clear early on that the sixth hole would be his signature hole. "Number six will, no doubt, play tough due to the paspalum grass we'll be planting," he explained. "That variety of grass becomes sticky when grown in tropical settings like Maui. Tee shots land and just stop. This will force players to hit long iron and even hybrid second shots, something most are not accustomed to doing."

Ava loved his enthusiasm. Clearly, he adored the game of golf. Even more, he adored creating courses that surprised and challenged even the most seasoned players.

Her phone buzzed, signaling an incoming text. She pulled it from her pocket to find a message from Elta. Alani's surgery had been scheduled. Day after tomorrow.

Ava suspected there was an urgency to the matter. No doubt, Evan had worked some magic to hasten the process. She was grateful.

Tom bent his head and gazed at her. "You sure you're okay?"

She couldn't hide the slight tremble in her hands as she

pocketed her phone. "Not entirely," she finally admitted. "My best friend, Alani Kané, is having surgery very soon to remove a cancerous growth in her breast. A very aggressive cancer. Unfortunately, she put off getting the lump checked, believing it to be nothing more than a fatty cyst, something her mother suffered. She was wrong."

Tom's deep blue eyes looked stricken. "Oh, Ava. I'm so very sorry. I really like both Elta and Alani. Elta's services at Wailea Chapel are very moving and Alani serves up the best luau around. Believe me, I checked them all out after moving to the island."

That brought a tiny smile to Ava's lips. "Yes, she does kalua pork like nobody else. It's famous, really."

Not entirely understanding what caused her to do so, she spilled. "I am just so worried, you know? Few people are as important to me as Alani is. She's my person. The one I can tell anything to. The friend who drops everything and comes, without me even having to ask."

She couldn't help it. She teared up.

"I...I just don't want to lose her. It would simply be too much after..." She paused. "Well, after everything that went on this past year." She'd leave it at that. There was no need to open up her wound and bleed all over him.

His hand reached for hers. He enfolded her fingers inside his warm, strong palm and squeezed. "I hope you know that whatever happens, I'll be there for you."

The admission seemed to surprise Tom as much as Ava. He quickly tried to recover. "I mean, you are a wonderful woman, Ava. You deserve all the support in the world."

His words, while unexpected, warmed her heart. At treacherous times like these, she intended to gather every offer of encouragement and reinforcement and would tuck them away in her heart waiting to pull the sentiments out for reinforcement when her own well ran dry. She'd already learned how few times she could handle the hard things alone. It took cherished friends and family walking alongside to prop her up.

Yes, Ava would gladly accept any support this new friend would lend. She gave Tom a warm and appreciative smile, well aware he had yet to let go of her hand.

24

"Willa, come on! We're going to be late!"

Willa sat on the edge of her bed with her attention glued to her phone, ignoring her mother's warnings.

Katie huffed. "Alani's surgery is this morning and I-am-not-going-to-be-late!" she repeated with a raised voice. "Move it...or get grounded."

Jon popped onto the scene carrying Noelle on his hip. Their dog, Givey, circled at his feet. "Willa, do as your mother asked, please."

Their daughter looked up and nodded. She tossed her phone on the bed and headed for her bathroom. "I'll be down in a minute."

As Jon and Katie turned and headed for the stairs, Katie narrowed her eyes and looked over at her husband. "Why does she do that?"

"Do what?"

"Why does she totally ignore me and the minute you show up on the scene, she's all 'Okay, Daddy. Sure...anything you ask.'"

Jon shook his head. "You exaggerate."

"Sure, Daddy. Sure, Daddy," little Noelle mimicked.

Katie chucked their toddler under her chin. "Oh, not you too."

With Jon's help, breakfast was consumed, daughters were dressed and loaded in his car. Just before pulling out of the driveway, he rolled down his window. "I love you."

Katie nodded. "I know you do."

"Are you sure you don't want me to go with you? I can still make arrangements at the restaurant," he offered.

Her husband was well aware how she had tossed and turned all night anticipating what the day would bring. Not only was their dear family friend facing surgery—they were all worried about what the surgeons might find—but this would be the first day any of them had faced Mia since the horrible discovery of her betrayal.

Katie had played the scene over in her mind a thousand times. What was she going to say? Would she even be able to say anything? They'd always been so close. Nothing would have prepared Katie for the blow Mia landed in the middle of her gut.

No matter which way she turned the scenario over in her mind, there was no good outcome. Hard things were just that...hard.

AIDEN LEFT the station feeling completely exhausted. He had been awake nearly twenty-four hours after working back-to-back rescues. The first was a vehicle extraction where an older couple were trapped after rolling their car. It had begun to rain lightly the night before which caused the roads to be slicker than normal. The elderly man had accidently hit the gas pedal instead of the brakes when rounding a corner.

The second rescue call came from a frantic mom who needed immediate help when her toddler escaped his crib in the middle of the night. The little guy somehow pulled out the drawers in a chest and climbed up. The heavy piece of furniture toppled over, pinning him underneath. When the mom heard the sudden noise, she came running to find her little boy was unconscious. Because of her proximity to the station, his team was the first to arrive. Last he'd heard, the tyke was going to be fine.

The mother, however, didn't fare as well. She was a mess and blamed herself for the unfortunate accident. By the time he'd spent some time reassuring her that unfortunate things happen...even under good mothers' watches, she finally quit crying.

That was what Aiden loved most about his job...he loved connecting with people and helping them through difficult and emotional situations. He was good at it. He was levelheaded and had a way of calming even the most volatile individuals, many of whom faced very scary circumstances.

Given that, you'd think he would not be so nervous about what his family faced today.

He'd spent an inordinate amount of time pondering what this day would be like for his mom. Facing Mia would be a knife to the heart. Add the tension of Alani's surgery, and you might as well twist that knife a thousand times over.

One thing for sure...he would do everything in his power to protect his mom and be by her side every step of the way.

Shane hated conflict. Why battle crappy situations when you could just move on? Even with Mia showing up and the family having to see her again after all that happened, what was the point of making such a big deal of it?

Sure, his mom still stung over what Mia did. But really, it was his dad's fault, wasn't it? He was the one who was married, the one who had promised for life and all that. Some days, Shane still wished for just a few minutes with him. He'd punch him in the face, then walk away and forget about it.

His sisters definitely felt much different. Aiden, too, in some ways. His siblings' feelings were all over the place on the matter. Personally, he didn't see the point of getting riled up. No one could go back and change anything. Why stir things up?

Besides, it wasn't like he'd always made the best choices.

The only thing a person could do was to admit you'd messed up and do better going forward. At least, that's the way he saw things.

CHRISTEL DRUMMED her fingers on the steering wheel while waiting at the red light. She dreaded today in so many ways.

Mia had been her best friend growing up. While unrelated, in some ways, they were like cousins. Their families often celebrated special occasions and holidays together. She'd spent as much time at the Kané house as she had her own. Likewise, Mia had slept over more times than Christel could even count.

That's what made all of this worse.

Christel's father hadn't just betrayed her mother and slept with just anyone...he slept with Mia. The thought of it still made her feel sick.

She couldn't even imagine how her mother must feel. Especially knowing she had to face her husband's mistress face-to-face today.

She hoped Mia thought it all worth it. Her actions had nearly destroyed two families: the Briscoes and the Kanés.

Christel wanted justice. She wanted Mia to pay for what

she'd done. Like a coward, she simply left, never even bothering to try to make amends.

Yes, Christel wanted justice. Somehow, Christel suspected that proper retribution would never come.

25

The day Ava had both dreaded and anticipated was here. Try as she might, she couldn't seem to build a barrier in her brain to ward off painful memories.

More than once, her mind drifted back to childhood...to that awful day when her dad came home and entered the living room, hat in hand. His eyes were flooded with tears as he knelt down in front of her and Vanessa, drawing their little girl hands into his own.

"I have bad news," he managed, his voice choking out each word as if it were a razor blade in this throat. "Your mom fought a good battle. She very much wanted to stay with us. God had something different in mind and took her to be with Him early this morning."

A horn honked behind her. Ava looked up to see the light had changed. She swallowed and pressed her foot down on the gas pedal and headed for the entrance to the airport where she would be meeting all four of her kids. Together, they would make the short flight to Honolulu and head to the hospital where they would meet up with Elta, Ori...and Mia.

Alani had checked into the hospital the night before in

order to go through all the pre-surgical preparations. That effort would continue this morning until the surgery, which was scheduled for right after lunchtime.

Perhaps she shouldn't have let her expectations for the initial biopsy results to run so high. True, she was the one who urged Alani to go and have the lump checked. It was the wise thing to do. Yet, Ava secretly hoped Alani's evaluation, that the lump was simply fatty tissue, was true.

Sadly, they'd learned the prognosis was far more dire.

Cancer.

Even the word caused Ava's blood to run cold.

Since learning the biopsy showed the worst, it seemed like Alani walked around with an imaginary surgical scalpel hanging around her neck. Nothing was normal...nor would it be for a long time.

Ava hated with every ounce of her being that her dear friend must face a very invasive procedure. Good case scenario would be a lumpectomy. Dr. Hinske warned no one would know until the surgeon was in there and could better assess the extent of growth as to whether or not a full mastectomy would be warranted.

Regardless, Ava wanted to be able to see Alani and hug her tight before she went for the procedure.

The airport parking lot was nearly full. It took several trips around the parking garage to find a spot and park. Ava gathered her purse and jacket and darted for the tram that would deliver her the short distance to the terminal.

She never seemed to get over the aroma in the air, which was especially strong here at the airport. It was as if the groundskeepers planted extra plumeria, hibiscus and Madagascar jasmine just so visitors to the area would have their senses delighted the minute they stepped from their planes.

Inside the terminal, Ava quickly made her way to the designated gate where her family waited.

"Mom, what took you so long?" Christel demanded. "Our flight leaves in minutes."

"I'm sorry," Ava apologized. "Traffic."

Her excuse wasn't entirely the truth, but close. In actuality, Ava woke feeling totally discombobulated and couldn't seem to get it together. She was lucky to have arrived when she did, given her mental state.

After exchanging greetings and hugs, they all got in line and handed their tickets to the ticket agent, then scrambled onto the jet bridge. They found their seats and buckled up. Minutes later, the plane took off exactly at the scheduled time.

When they landed in Honolulu, Aiden herded them to the rental car. Within a half hour, they were at the entrance of Queen's Medical Center where Alani was to have her surgery.

As they stepped into the lobby, a massive entrance to the medical facility that rivaled lobbies of some of the most upscale hotels on the islands. While buzzing with activity, the décor had a serene feel with sea colors in blues and greens and upholstered furniture arranged in conversational groupings. Opulent chandeliers hung from a soaring ceiling above polished flooring leading to a bank of elevators. One might mistakenly believe it to be a grand hotel lobby if not for the telltale voices coming from overhead speakers. *"Paging, Dr. Soros."*

Ava glanced at her watch. "Look, it's a couple of hours before Alani's surgery. It might be best if you go directly to the cafeteria and grab a bite to eat before heading upstairs. This might be your only opportunity for a real meal in several hours."

"What about you?" Katie asked.

Ava's hand covered her stomach. "I couldn't eat, even if I wanted to."

Christel nodded. "We'll bring something up to you, just in case you change your mind."

Ava kissed her daughter's cheek. "Thanks, honey." She gave

Katie, Aiden, and Shane quick hugs too. "I'll see you all upstairs."

She stood and watched them go, then turned and headed for the elevators. The medi-surgical floors were on the fifth floor.

The elevator doors opened and Ava stepped inside. She reached for the bank of buttons as the doors slid shut. Suddenly an arm stopped the doors from closing and a woman stepped inside, joining Ava.

Ava looked up, prepared to greet the person. Her heart stopped.

It was Mia Kané.

26

Despite promising herself she would face Lincoln's mistress with strength and dignity, feelings of panic immediately engulfed her like a rising tide, wave after wave coming so fast that Ava struggled to breathe.

From the look on Mia's face, she experienced something similar. "Hello, Ava," she said, the color lifting from her dark complexion. Her fingers were trembling.

What seemed like an eternity passed as they stood there staring. In actuality, only a second or two ticked away before Ava turned to her. "Mia."

She'd wanted to say more. The words wouldn't come.

What did come was a wave of unexpected resentment. She had worked so hard to move past Lincoln's betrayal and had purposed to live with joy...to embrace peace and not let the actions of others pull her under.

This was still her intent. Ava had not expected her emotions to betray her.

She dropped her gaze and stared at her own shoes, wishing she was anywhere but standing next to her husband's mistress with the heaviness of betrayal robbing the air of oxygen.

The elevator chugged upward, taking its sweet time arriving on the fifth floor. Eventually, a ding sounded and the doors slid open.

Ava hung back and let Mia exit first. She then followed.

They immediately stepped into the surgical waiting room, a bright and cheery area with windows providing views of tall swaying palms and gardens filled with colorful flowers. According to the internet, the hospital had recently undergone a renovation funded by an anonymous donor, someone who obviously had substantial assets...and generosity.

In order to escape the tension, Ava focused on the décor: modern with lots of woods and sectional sofas with bright green fabric. Vending machines had been replaced with an extensive coffee bar lined with Keurig machines and bowls filled with individually-wrapped granola bars, bags of nuts and fresh fruit. A pretty box with a slit on top was there for donations.

Across the room stood Elta and Ori. As Mia approached, they gave her tight hugs. Ava so wanted to go over and ask Elta for recent news. She held back wanting to give them a moment. Of course, she wasn't anxious to be near Mia if she didn't have to be.

Some people she recognized from Wailea Chapel were talking near the windows. She greeted them with a little wave. It was really nice that they had come to support their pastor and his family.

Ava went and got herself a cup of coffee and shoved a couple of bills in the little box. Before she could turn, she felt a hand on her shoulder. She turned to find Elta beside her.

"I know this is hard for you, Ava," he said softly, pointing out the obvious. Hard didn't begin to cover her emotions. His daughter's presence was excruciating.

Even so, she pushed her own feelings aside and drew him into a hug. This man meant the world to her. "How's Alani? I'm anxious to see her." She offered him the coffee she'd just made. "Any news from the medical team this morning?"

He took the coffee. "The surgery is still scheduled for early afternoon. She had lab tests done last night and more this morning. They hooked her up to an IV and she was told the surgeon would be in to talk to us right after he finished up his morning scheduled procedures. In fact, I should get back. I just wanted to..." He let his voice drift off.

Of course, he wanted to come out and greet his daughter. Mia had been gone for nearly a year.

He grabbed her hand. "I know the difficulties all this presents, but would you please go back with us? Alani was asking for you this morning."

Ava's will softened. "Of course, I'll do anything for Alani. Anything at all."

It hit her then that the one thing most important before her...the one action that would most benefit her best friend this morning would be for Ava to set aside her own hurts and at least be kind to her daughter.

Ava lifted her chin. It would be terribly hard, but she could do that.

For Alani.

With that determination tucked inside, Ava followed her best friend's family through the doors leading to the patient rooms, down the shiny floors and past a busy nurses' station.

Elta stopped in front of a closed door. "This is it," he reported. He turned to Mia. "Your mom is very anxious to see you, sweetheart."

Mia teared up causing her brother to take her hand. "We're glad you're here," Ori told her.

The tender exchange brought a tiny smile to Ava's lips. Despite the events of last year, this family was like her own. Ori and Mia had been raised alongside her own children. She couldn't imagine it, but if Christel had done what Mia had, she knew Alani's faith would help her forgo her own feelings and do everything in her power to offer redemption. It's what she adored about Alani.

It was at that moment that a tiny prayer went up, a bargain of sorts with her maker.

Don't take Alani from me and I will forgive her daughter...of even that.

27

Fortified with full stomachs, the Briscoe siblings made their way upstairs to join their mom. When they stepped off the elevator, it became immediately evident that Ava, Elta, and Ori were not there. Neither was Mia.

"Where do you suppose they are?" Katie asked, immediately concerned.

Christel joined her in that concern. She glanced around, scowling. "I'm not sure."

Mrs. Olson, a woman who attended Wailea Chapel, stepped forward. "They all went in to see Alani," she reported, then shook her head. "A person just can't ignore their health. Last year, I discovered an abscess on my leg. Dang thing popped up overnight. It was hot and oozed with drainage. An awful thing."

She pulled herself up straight. "My son told me to ignore it. Said most of these types of things go away on their own." She poked the air with her forefinger. "Well, I am happy to report I followed my gut. Went to a local urgent care. They took one look and sent me to the ER." She shook her head again, this time making a tsking sound. "It was infected. Severely infected. Had I not had the good sense to have it checked, I might have lost my leg." She grabbed a banana from a basket on the coffee bar and went to work peeling the skin back. "Only a fool ignores things like that." She shoved the banana in her mouth and took a bite. While chewing, she added, "Only a fool."

Katie cringed. Everyone wished the diagnosis had come much earlier, but pointing fingers at their friend's health sensibilities was of no good now.

She turned to Aiden. "You hungry?"

He looked at her like she had two heads. "We just had breakfast."

Katie sighed. "True, but I thought maybe..." She let her voice drift as she looked around the nicely decorated room. She especially loved the wall colors, a pretty shade of light green and sky blue. Oblong prints lined the wall behind the receptionist desk. Matching furniture and lighting finished the look.

She pulled out her phone and pointed it toward the cylinder-shaped chandeliers made of wood.

"What are you doing?" Christel hissed under her breath.

"I'm taking pictures. I want to email these to Jasmit Tan, our former architect. He'd appreciate this style. I'm sure it's no coincidence that the colorful paintings, murals, and photographs decorating this space were carefully chosen." She clicked off a few shots. "Research has shown that art has the power to heal. Many of the images represented in this artwork will calm patients and families waiting to hear news of their loved ones' health. It reduces stress."

Christel rolled her eyes. "Whatever." She turned to Shane. "So, you think Mom went up there with her...alone?"

"Her?" he asked, looking confused. "Oh, you mean Mia?"

"Of course, I mean Mia," she confirmed, her voice clearly exasperated. "Who else would I mean?"

Katie knew what Shane meant. Mia wasn't the only female here to support Alani. She wanted to step up and tell Christel that. The look on her sister's face made her rethink the need to.

Aiden wandered to the bank of windows. "I heard the weatherman on the radio forecast an incoming storm later this week." He shook his head and laughed. "That bright sunshine hints he might have been wrong."

Katie joined him. "I remember when you were younger, you thought about being a weather guy."

"A meteorologist," he corrected. "The field of meteorology aims to understand and predict the earth's atmospheric phenomena, including the weather. They are highly skilled in using mathematical models and knowledge to prepare forecasts that are often very accurate."

Katie shrugged. "Yeah, a weatherman."

Mrs. Olson came up between the two of them and wedged into their conversation. "The weather is an absolute bear on my arthritis." She rubbed her knuckles. "My joints can tell when the weather is going to change, sometimes days ahead."

She looked between Katie and Aiden. "Young people have no idea what it is like to get old. No idea at all. Some days I can barely walk when I get out of bed. Swollen ankles, aching toe joints, and all those inflamed tissues under my heel...goodness, brings tears to my eyes."

The white-haired woman fingered the bun at the back of her head. "Don't even try to imagine what aging does to your intestinal system. I've never had constipation like I have had in the past six months. And then when the good Lord finally gives me some relief, well...look out. No one had better come in that bathroom for hours."

Katie stifled a giggle. She knew Aiden was super sensitive when it came to even a hint of foul smells. The entire family found it puzzling how he could face injuries, blood and gore in his job, yet wretch uncontrollably when Shane purposely passed gas as he walked by. Yes, her brothers were fully grown... and still children.

"Uh, excuse me," Aiden said, begging off and leaving the conversation. He darted for the men's restroom.

Mrs. Olson patted Katie's arm. "The church's women's auxiliary has been praying for favor for the pastor's wife. Alani has never been ill a day in her life, to my knowledge." She shook her head. "This is such an awful thing."

Katie extracted herself as graciously as she could and made her way to Christel. "So, Mom's likely up there with Mia."

Christel said nothing. She simply nodded.

"Who do you think did this renovation? I mean, they did a good job. It takes a professional with a gift for design to create such an inviting environment. You would barely know it camouflages so much illness and heartache." She glanced at her sister's nearly empty coffee cup. "Want some more coffee?"

Without waiting for a reply, she lifted the cup from Christel's hand, walked over to the coffee bar and tossed the empty cup in the trash. She pulled a clean one and positioned it under the Keurig then took on the task of selecting a coffee pod. There were so many flavors.

When the coffee had brewed, she carried the cup back to Christel. "Here you go."

Christel murmured, "Thank you."

Katie took the seat next to her sister. "I really like that color of blue on the wall. It looks like the sky early in the morning." She pointed up to the cavernous ceiling. "Especially with the lighting. I love how they combined the canned lights with the pretty hanging wood cylinders."

Christel grunted. "Would you shut up?"

Katie turned. "What?"

"Please, I know you're nervous. We all are. But can we just quit with the architectural review?"

Katie's feelings smarted. "Well, sure. Fine."

Christel sighed. "Oh, don't get all out of sorts. I didn't mean to hurt your feelings. I've just got a lot on my mind." She took a sip from the coffee. "How long do you think Mom's going to be up there?"

They looked up to find Ori walking toward them in the waiting area.

"How's your mom, Ori?" Christel asked.

"Her spirits are up, despite what she faces." He took a deep breath. "Mom wanted Ava to stay while they talked to the surgeon." When they didn't ask, he added, "Mia, too. I just... well, I needed to get of there." His eyes filled with tears.

Christel immediately drew his shoulders into a tight hug. "Your mom is going to be all right, Ori. Evan lined her up with the best care possible. This medical team knows what they are doing and will guide her through this."

Katie patted him on the back. "Yes, people beat breast cancer all the time. Alani will, too."

He looked at them both miserably. "Yeah? How do you know?"

Katie motioned in the direction of Mrs. Olson and her group. "Because, from what I hear, the women's auxiliary has been asking God for a miracle."

28

Ava sat by Alani's hospital bed and drew her best friend's hand into her own. "Are you nervous?" Both Elta and Mia were over by the windows on their phones.

Alani looked at Ava and squeezed her hand. "Yes," she admitted. "I'm afraid I'm fighting a lot of emotions this morning. Still, I'm doing my best to remain upbeat." She motioned in the direction of her family. "For them. You saw how Ori left the room fighting tears. We are a family of faith and know God remains in control, but this is hard. Especially the unknown." Her hand drifted to her breast. "I only wish I knew what was ahead."

Ava nodded. "No matter what you face, I'm right here by your side. I won't leave."

Alani's face filled with emotion. "You are my best friend, Ava. My Jonathan," she said, referring to a well-known Bible story about David and his close friend. "I know how very hard it is for you to be here." While she didn't point out the obvious, they both knew she was referring to Mia.

Ava remembered her bargain with God. Setting her rocks

down would be a small price to pay for Alani's restored health. "You just focus on getting well." Ava gave her best friend's hand another tight squeeze.

The door opened and in strode a short man with a hawkish nose. He pulled a surgical cap from his head. "Hello, I'm Dr. Barry Hinske. Sorry I've not been able to come meet you all before this." Without waiting for a reply, he pulled out what looked like an iPad and pressed the screen. Immediately an illuminated reader box mounted on the wall lit up with Alani's x-ray image. Dr. Hinske studied the image several seconds before pointing to a dark gray area. "This is our trouble area," he told them. "And see these?" His finger shifted to several more spots. "These are what we're most concerned about. There are a lot of tiny spots though out the breast tissue, many appear to be recent growths." He leaned closer for a better look. "Yes, I can tell by the lighter shade."

He turned to them. "The tests I ordered that you took last night and this morning will tell me even more."

His face softened a tiny bit as he looked to Alani. "Evan tells me you have a family history of these kinds of lumps." Again, without waiting for a reply, he extended his hand and took her hand. "I promise you have come to the right hospital and I'm the right doctor to give you the best opportunity to beat this." He went on to tell them about himself including his training and experience.

He reiterated that there were areas in the scans that caused concern, but that the surgery would clarify the situation.

When Mia questioned the doctor about the possibility of a lumpectomy instead of a full mastectomy, Dr. Hinske said it certainly was a possibility, but that he wanted to make that decision in the operating room. Given what appeared to be the advanced stage of cancer in the larger mass, the placement, and the palpable size of the lump, he suspected there may be some lymph node involvement. He would remove some of the nodes and send them to the lab during surgery. Those results would help him determine what procedures to do.

"Alani," Dr. Hinske spoke gently now. "I want you to be prepared to wake up from surgery and face either option—the lumpectomy or the mastectomy."

Alani nodded solemnly.

"I know this is all happening very fast. But I want you to know my entire team is on your side. We're going to do the best we can to make sure you have a good outcome."

Dr. Hinske shut off the x-ray image. He grabbed a pen from his front scrubs pocket and made a note in the stack of documents attached to a clipboard before folding it under his arm. "Any more questions?"

Of course they had questions...dozens. But, none of them voiced them. Instead, they all thanked the surgeon and watched as he exited the room.

Everyone remained silent. After several seconds, Elta finally moved to his wife's bedside. He started to say something about trusting God, but choked mid-sentence. Ori and Mia both rushed to his side and enfolded him in their arms. Mia bent and kissed her mother's cheek, clearly struggling to maintain her composure. "I'm sure it's going to turn out just fine, Mom. You'll see."

Ava wanted to join in and express her own confidence that all would be well in the end. Each time she tried to open her mouth to offer encouragement, an image of her own mother appeared.

Ava knew there were no promises. So instead, she simply pursed her lips and hoped for the best.

29

"You have all been promoted to a very special assignment—working on what we call *Operation Mai Tai*. Everything that is said, all that is learned and discovered in this room, stays in this room. No deviation. Understood?" Vanessa glanced around at the somber looks on the faces of the small group gathered around the battered folding table. She waited until they all nodded before continuing. "Our work will be critical to Jim's campaign and successful run, not only in the primaries, but on into the general. It is in this hub that we'll be uncovering and dissecting what we hope will be the mother lode of information: highly confidential material that could make or break this upcoming election."

Scott BeVier lifted his eyebrows. "Why is it called Operation Mai Tai?"

Vanessa grinned. "Because we're hoping people will get loose-lipped, like when they down alcohol."

With an almost giddy anticipation, she explained that as members of the special apparatus for tracking and research, they would be watching hours of broadcasted speeches by Jim Kahele's primary opponent and reading blogs and online news articles, sifting for any critical piece of data that might catch him flip-flopping on an earlier position, misquoting facts, or generally making snafus that could be spun in the media. They were told to especially watch for anything that would tip a change in strategy in Jim's camp, even if slight.

"Aren't there political oppo outfits we could hire to do this?"

Vanessa gave him an impatient look. "Yes, but my years in media taught me one very critical lesson...do not rely on others to find the important stuff. Dig up your own information. Ferret out people in the know and get them to talk. That's how you find the gold, the nuggets no one else has."

She took a sip from her coffee cup. "Understand?"

They all nodded.

Kickback, their ragtag IT guy, handed off an electronic device into Vanessa's hand. "This should record anything you need...undetected."

She nodded with satisfaction, then turned back to her team. "Don't discount anything," she told them. "Trust your gut. If you think something might be important, it usually is."

Lucille, Jim's mother, slowly removed her glasses and wiped the lenses with a cloth she retrieved from her back pocket. With her frames back in place, she looked over the room, appearing skeptical as she returned to petting Axel.

Vanessa suspected she might immediately run and report all this to Jim. Let her. This is exactly why Jim hired her. Her skills at investigative reporting put her in a top anchor chair. This is where she excelled.

She lifted her chin and went on. "We'll be working in shifts and will meet briefly twice a day to download to the rest of the team what we've learned. You'll be provided a written report via a daily email, incorporating data we've gathered." She pointed to the device Kickback had given to her. "Everything on this special server is encrypted, and nothing can be printed or downloaded. Any questions?"

No one raised a hand. Scott BeVier looked bored and tapped his pencil against the top of the table.

Vanessa wanted to grab that pencil and break it.

Anyone willing to make the effort could look in the public record and assemble information—but you couldn't manufacture incentive inside people who didn't want to put in the effort.

This was important. She didn't have the financial resources to hire anyone else. She was stuck with the staff they had.

Some might even argue this effort was overkill. Especially here at the primary level. As a former news anchor, she had covered many campaigns. People often overlooked the fact that it was prior to the actual election where mistakes were often made...mistakes that came back to haunt candidates.

If, and when, that happened—she wanted the campaign to capture that mistake and make the most of it.

This campaign was her chance to redeem herself after being fired from the news station.

She fully intended to make sure Jim Kahele won this election.

30

Ava sat in the surgical waiting room with the others, mindlessly staring at the television mounted on the wall. Her mind felt like Jell-O as she rehearsed all the things Dr. Hinske had said before Alani was taken back for surgery.

The initial biopsy results had not been good prompting the need for further medical intervention. Dr. Hinske had made it clear that a total mastectomy was possible. Her heart broke for her friend. This option would extend recovery and incur additional emotional consequences. Still, she fully agreed with Dr. Hinske. They would not want to take chances leaving any stray cells in there.

Aiden folded into the seat beside her and handed her a hot cup of coffee. "Thought you could use this," he offered.

"Thank you, sweetheart." Ava took the cup and took a welcome sip when her phone dinged, signaling an incoming text.

"*Thinking about you. I hope all goes well with your friend.*"

Aiden leaned over. "Who's that?"

Ava couldn't help it. A tiny smile nipped at the corner of her mouth. "Tom Strobe, the architect who is working on the golf course renovation."

Her oldest son lifted his brows. "That was nice of him."

Ava nodded. "Yes, he's a very nice guy."

Ava felt herself tremble as her thoughts turned back to Alani. "You know what Alani did as they wheeled her down the hall?"

Aiden shook his head. "No, what?"

"She clutched her breast with one hand and held the other hand high above her head, pointing to heaven."

Her son patted her leg. "She's right. God has got this."

"I know," she muttered, not adding what was playing inside her mind. God may have this, but not one day was promised here on earth. Suffering was a part of life. He took people home all the time.

Elta and Mia entered the waiting room, pulling everyone's attention.

Christel was standing near and Ava could hear her nearly snarl. She quickly gave her daughter a warning look.

She'd had the talk with all of her children. As uncomfortable as it would be to face Mia, there would be no drama. No confrontation. They were here to support Alani.

Katie was the first to cross the line and forgo her request... well, sort of.

She pointed to a program on the television, a talk show featuring a celebrity who had just been outed for an affair while married. "Oh, look!" Katie exclaimed. "Another of *those* women." She turned and stared at Mia.

Shane quickly took his sister by the elbow and lifted her from her seat. "Let's take a walk."

Despite minor protests, he guided her through the waiting room and out into the hall.

Christel glanced over at her mother and then dropped her gaze to the floor.

Ava knew how hard it was for her daughter to not follow suit with her younger sister and fire some of her anger at Mia. She didn't blame her kids. They were terribly hurt by Mia's actions. It was only natural to want justice.

As Elta has preached so many times, true justice was the Lord's. For her own mental sake, she rehearsed that sentiment dozens of times a day...especially lately knowing she had to see Mia again. She hoped her kids might do the same.

What could be said really?

Were there any words, any accusations made with a harsh tone that would erase the situation and make everything right again? No. All they could do was focus on Alani and get past today as mentally intact as possible.

Ava remembered her bargain with God.

She meant every word of that promise. Forgiving Alani's daughter would be a small thing in trade for her best friend's life.

That's when she noticed Shane walk across the room with two cups of coffee in his hands. He headed for Elta and Mia and handed them each a cup.

When his hands were free, he patted Elta on the back and said something Ava couldn't quite make out. Shane then turned his full attention to Mia. Saying nothing, he simply reached and touched her arm. Then he walked away.

Sometimes the strongest message didn't require words.

AVA MET Alani Kané years ago at a Little League game. Their sons were new to the game and both of the mothers were new to the chaos created from fitting multiple practices and games into their already full schedules.

Ava sat on the bleachers, second bench from the bottom with her hands shading her eyes. Aiden had lost interest in the game at hand and was picking weeds from the grass and placing them inside his baseball cap. She stood and frantically motioned, trying to get his attention.

"Aiden, honey...listen to the coach," she hollered.

Out of the corner of her eye, she saw a large woman lumber across the field heading in their direction. The woman wore a bright colored floral dress...well, a muumuu, really. Few women could pull that look off, but Alani strode across the grass looking like Hawaiian royalty, chin up and big round black sunglasses parked on her nose. She pulled a cooler on wheels. A folded sun umbrella was tucked under the other arm. A massive beach bag was strapped over her shoulder.

As she approached the bleachers, she waved. "What have I missed?" she asked the gaggle of moms.

The only space available with a spot big enough for her ample behind was next to Ava. She settled her belongings and wedged in, looked her way, and said, "Hi, I'm Alani."

Ava grinned. "I'm Ava."

Her new friend rarely let a quiet moment pass. If she wasn't yelling in the direction of the field, she was chattering about her latest attempt at the perfect Kahlua pork. "I'm planning on opening a commercial luau. It's going to be grand."

Ava loved her confidence.

They became fast and furious friends that day, spending subsequent days together any time the opportunity presented. They introduced their husbands, shared backyard picnics, traded babysitting, and shared names of good doctors and dentists.

Ava had never had a close female friend.

Alani soon became her close confidante. She could share anything with her friend, always had...doubts, fears, and dreams. Even the unfortunate event with Mia and Lincoln failed to create a wedge between them. They were glued together with a relationship bond that could never be broken.

She hated that Christel and Mia's friendship was fractured, perhaps permanently. It took a lot to get Christel on your bad side, but once you landed in her bad column, she crossed you off her balance sheet.

This was why Ava found herself holding her breath when she saw Mia make a few tentative steps in Christel's direction.

CHRISTEL'S HEART pounded as she saw Mia walking toward her. She quickly glanced around hoping to find an exit to the situation, graceful or not. Yet, something kept her feet planted and she didn't move.

"Christel," Mia said, softly.

Christel found it hard to breathe. Unable to push out a reply, she simply nodded.

"Thank you for being here," Mia said. "I know how much it means to my mom."

"Of course I'd be here," Christel said, the words cutting the tense air like little razor blades. "Your mother means a lot to our family."

They both stood and stared, unsure who should take the next step, say the next thing. Finally, Mia opened her mouth. "Mom told me you got married."

Christel nodded. "Yes."

Mia shuffled on her feet. "Congratulations. I'm really happy for you."

Mia had been one of her closest allies as Christel walked through the pain of Jay's addiction. It was easy to count on both hands, and more, the times Christel had shown up at Mia's place and talked into the wee hours of the morning, seeking advice and solace. Mia never seemed to judge. She was always supportive. "You alone will know what to do and when to do it," she kept saying. "I trust your judgment, Christel."

The morning of the day her divorce from Jay became final, Mia rang her doorbell holding a box of donuts and a bottle of bubble bath. "I'm here to remind you to be good to yourself today."

Christel looked over at her former friend and felt her throat choking up with anger. "Yes, Mia. I got married." She flashed her hand and wedding ring. "For some of us, marriage is a legal bond and spiritual covenant that matters."

She knew her words were mean. She didn't care.

Mia barely flinched. "I agree. Marriage matters," she said, her words barely above a whisper.

"Really?" Christel looked at her incredulously. "Call up the media. That's certainly news to the Briscoe family."

Tears immerged in Mia's eyes. "I—I'm more sorry than you'll ever know."

"Sorry? And that is supposed to make everything better? Sorry, and that fixes what you did?"

Mia shook her head. "I know it doesn't fix anything."

Christel's voice raised. "You're damn right, it doesn't fix anything. You sliced my mother in two!"

Aiden appeared by his sister's side. He took Christel by the arm. "Not the time or place."

Christel angrily pulled her arm from his clutches. "No, of course not. I can't imagine a time when I can ever look at her and think anything but horrific thoughts. She's a traitor."

Ava stood. It was time to shut this down.

Before she could make a move, Dr. Hinske appeared.

"Elta, could I see you and your daughter?" He pointed to a tiny room behind a closed door off to the right. "Alone?"

Elta immediately grabbed Christel's mom by the hand. "Ava's coming too," he said, firmly.

Dr. Hinske nodded. "Fine."

They all watched as Dr. Hinske led them into that room.

31

Dr. Hinske closed the door and invited them to take a seat. He folded onto the end of a small sofa and turned pages on a clipboard. He cleared his throat. "The surgery went well," he reported. "As feared, we did have to do a complete mastectomy. The largest tumor was deeply embedded in the chest wall, and I wanted to make certain we got it all. The added smaller masses only confirmed that was the correct approach." He glanced down the page. "We removed a number of lymph nodes—eleven, to be exact. It seemed to me, visually, that there was migration into the lymph system, so I removed tissue well beyond what the involvement appeared, just to be on the safe side. I believe we got it all." He looked up at Elta. "Alani responded very well to the surgery. We kept a close monitor and suffered no issues with her heart." He had warned Alani's weight might cause some cardiac-related consequences while under anesthesia for an extended time.

This time he directed his attention to Mia. "Your mother will be waking shortly. The nurse will change the dressing on the surgical area soon, and then again every few hours. Even though we warned Alani what was possible, the news will come as a shock. Ultimately, I think she will be pleased with how smooth the surgical site is and that the scarring will be minimal, once the incision heals."

Elta took a deep breath. "What are we looking at? Going forward?" His voice sounded small.

Dr. Hinske's expression filled with compassion. "We won't know for sure until the lab confirms, but from every indication, I believe we're looking at stage IV."

Ava felt the air leave her lungs. "What...what does that mean?" She knew exactly what that could mean. She yearned for concrete confirmation that her worst fears would not be realized.

Dr. Hinske sobered. "Despite the late stage, this is not the death sentence it once was. Sure, we wish the cancer had been discovered earlier. Still, this cancer is treatable. We'll hit it with everything we've got."

Ava felt as though she'd turned into a statue. A freezing feeling swept through her veins and she shuddered with a sudden chill. "Radiation?"

Dr. Hinske nodded. "And aggressive chemotherapy. I know this was not what we were hoping to find, but now that we know what we're dealing with, our team of oncologists will put all their collective knowledge and resources to work on beating this thing." He gathered his clipboard and stood. "We have every reason to believe Alani will do just fine."

It wasn't until after the surgeon left the room that Ava caught his deliberate phrasing. There was a big difference between Alani *doing* fine...and *being* fine.

AVA STEPPED inside the darkened hospital room. Everyone had left the hospital, including Elta and Mia. She'd urged her kids to get them out of the hospital for a quick break and to get dinner.

The day had been a long one. Nerves had been on high throughout the hours of waiting. News of Dr. Hinske's prognosis only worsened the situation. Yes, she did believe the notion that this wasn't a certain death sentence. Yet, any way you looked at this critical health issue, Alani was headed for a severe fight that would alter her life...at least in the near term.

Alani would have to push every ounce of her being toward the battle. Other, more minor, circumstances would also plague her friend...loss of her breast would create a mental fight on its own, including dealing with loss of hair, loss of strength, and intense pain as the muscles and incisions healed. The impact would be substantial.

Ava knew one thing...she would walk this journey with her friend.

She looked around the room. Machines with blinking lights and beeps monitored Alani's heart and temperature. There were drainage bags and bandages. Nurses came in and out, checking on Alani and reviewing the digital reports on the monitors.

In a rare moment of solitude, Alani started to wake.

Ava quickly leaned over her friend. "I'm here, Alani. How are you, sweet friend?"

Alani lifted her eyes open slowly. She moved her mouth as though there was cotton pasted to her tongue. "Where is everyone?" she managed to ask in a raspy voice.

Ava explained that her family was with Christel, Aiden, Katie, and Shane. "They and the group from Wailea Chapel all went out for some dinner," she quietly explained.

"Good," Alani murmured. "Elta needs to eat."

Ava tucked the covers in around her friend. "Are you hurting? Do I need to call your nurse?"

Alani's drooping eyes reminded Ava strong narcotics were

likely flowing into Alani's veins via the IV attached to her arm. No doubt, she'd be drifting off to sleep again very soon.

Ava reached and swept her hand softly across her best friend's cheek. Choking back tears, she bit her lip. "I love you, Alani. I want you to know that. No person has been there for me more than you. No one knows my heart more than you. I...I just want you to know how very much you mean to me." She couldn't go on. Her constricted throat kept any further words from coming.

Surprisingly, Alani became alert. She opened her eyes and looked over at Ava, grabbed her hand and squeezed. "I love you too, Ava."

Ava sniffed and ventured to ask the question she knew her best friend would voice, had they changed places. She extended an invitation to bare her heart, and the real feelings buried within. "Are you scared?"

Alani shook her head slowly. "Oddly, no. I'm no longer frightened or even nervous." She squeezed Ava's hand a second time. "Healing...or heaven. That is what is ahead. And if healing does not come, I'm not afraid of the last aloha."

32

Christel sat curled up on the sofa eating chocolate cherry ice cream right out of the carton.

"Wow. Sounds like you had quite the day." Evan handed her a napkin. "Don't beat yourself up. Tensions were already high. It's understandable that you had a hard time keeping your emotions in check when it came to Mia."

She scooped another huge bite of ice cream and held it suspended in the air. "Yes, but I promised Mom. My outburst made things worse for her...let alone for Elta. I'm ashamed of myself."

She slipped the spoon inside her mouth, letting the ice cream feed her emotions.

Truth was, she had held back. Had she let herself do what she truly wanted, she would have smacked Mia right across the face.

Christel handed off the half-eaten carton of ice cream to her husband. "I guess this isn't helping."

He pulled the ice cream from her hand and moved for the kitchen. Upon returning, he took her chin into his hand and lifted her face to his. "I know there is a long string of people in your life who you loved but who hurt you deeply. I wish I could make that different. The only thing I can urge is that you quit looking back. Look forward...to our future."

He pulled her against him. She could hear his heartbeat, felt his warmth. "You can count on me. I will never intentionally cause you pain. In fact, I will do everything in my power to make you feel loved and secure. I'm used to repairing hurt places." He kissed the top of her head. "I'm good at it."

Christel felt her angst resolve.

Evan was right. Mia, her father, even Jay...they had all let her down. Some intentionally. Some by choice. Some because their foot would not step off a dangerous path.

The end result was all the same. Her soul was nicked and bleeding.

Seeing Mia today opened the wound. Pain gushed.

She took a deep breath and lifted her face to her own personal surgeon, the one who had slipped a ring on her finger and had promised to make her whole.

He kissed her deeply until she couldn't breathe anymore, couldn't claim to own even the smallest portion of her body. He took it all from her, forced her to want him with a desperation that was so intense it hurt.

Christel squeezed her eyes tightly closed and opened herself up shamelessly, both body and soul, crying out his name and clinging to him. Nothing mattered—not Mia, not her father, not Jay—only she and Evan and how alive he made her feel.

"What are you doing?" Katie screamed.

Her daughter's head popped up from behind the sofa cushions followed by a boy's head, his blond hair tousled and his face flushed.

"What in the pineapples and coconuts are you two doing?" she repeated, her own face growing red with anger. She handed off Noelle to Jon, who was standing behind her. "Here, take her," she barked before marching to the couch.

Willa scrambled up, smoothed her hair. "Mom, settle down. We weren't naked or anything. Geez...we were only kissing."

Katie glared at the boy. "Who are you?"

He, too, scrambled to his feet. "I—I'm Devon Connor." He attempted a weak smile. "We met...at the ballgame."

Katie immediately recalled then that this was the kid from the concession stand, the one Willa got all googly-eyed over.

She hadn't seen a car in front of the house. "How did you get here?" she demanded.

Her question met with silence as guilt formed in her daughter's face.

"Willa?" Jon said. "Answer your mother."

"I picked him up," Willa admitted, looking like she'd rather be a pig roasting over hot coals at Alani's luau than be standing here in front of her parents confessing what she'd done.

"You drove?" Katie asked, her eyes wide with incredulity. She pointed out the obvious. "You don't have a license."

"No lice, no lice," Noelle repeated.

Jon set his tiny daughter on the floor and handed her the television remote for diversion. She happily began pressing buttons.

Katie swore that mothering was an extreme sport. It's why she wore exercise clothes most days. She rolled her eyes and grabbed the remote from Noelle's dimpled hands as the television turned on and the sound blared.

Immediately, Noelle started to scream. Big crocodile-sized tears formed and rolled down her chubby cheeks.

Katie huffed and picked her up. She glared at Willa, then the boy. She turned to Jon. "Deal with them. I'm going to bed."

With that, she stomped up the fancy floating staircase and

headed for her younger daughter's room. She let the doors slam behind her.

Tears flowed as Katie laid Noelle down on the bed and unbuttoned her shirt. When she'd finished undressing her, she tucked her clothes under one arm and moved to the pretty salmon-colored dresser, pulled out a drawer, and retrieved a little nightgown—one with bears and fairies printed on the front.

The image brightened Noelle's spirits. She pointed. "Bear... bear." As she repeated the words it sounded more like beer, something Katie could use right now. A tall cold one with a foamy top in a frosted mug. She'd down it straight away and ask for a refill. Maybe she'd repeat the process several times until her mind grew foggy and the world felt soft and warm again.

Katie rehearsed the day's events as she dressed Noelle in her nighty and placed her inside her crib. She leaned and kissed the tiny girl on the forehead. "Go to sleep, Noelle. Mommy is tired."

As if understanding her mother was not in the mood for funny business, Noelle nodded and closed her eyes, then rolled over, pulling a stuffed turtle into her tiny arms and hugging it to her body.

Katie lifted the salmon-colored puff quilt up around her little girl. "Night, baby." She flicked off the light and headed back into the hall.

The open concept design allowed her to look down into the living area where Jon grabbed his keys and motioned for Devon to follow him. He was going to drive him home. Willa turned for the stairs.

Katie quickly ducked inside her own bedroom and quietly closed the door with her hip. She would speak with her daughter in the morning, sort all this out. She'd think of profound and motherly things to say, provide important lessons about being trustworthy and honest. She'd warn about the dangers of being deceptive, encourage her to reach now for the woman she wanted to be when she grew up.

Yes, she'd do all those things. But not tonight.

Tonight, she simply needed to put her head on the pillow, close her eyes and try to erase the past eighteen hours.

Alani had cancer...stage IV.

What would that mean? Worst case...well, she didn't even want to go there and what that would do to her mother and to their friends, Elta and Ori. While no longer considered a friend, she wouldn't wish that on Mia either.

Losing a close family member to death profoundly impacted every person in the circle. In their case, the loss had hit twice when the affair with Mia was uncovered.

Mia.

She seemed a stranger now. No longer the close childhood friend who played Barbies on the floor, the giggly high school chum who shared makeup tips and helped her curl her hair. Mia would never again be the girl Katie looked up to and wished to be more like.

Mia's choices changed everything. Unknowing to all of them, she had morphed into a box jellyfish, lurking beneath the Hawaiian water, her tentacles filled with barbed stingers that had sent her entire family into emotional shock, causing excruciating pain and gnarly scars.

Today, she stood there in the hospital waiting room as if none of this were true. As if all she'd done was nip at their ankles with a few sharp teeth.

Katie was glad Christel had let her have it, saying everything all of them wanted to shout. Nothing could make Katie claim otherwise.

Worse? Alani's cancer diagnosis meant Mia would be staying...perhaps indefinitely. The entire Briscoe family would be forced into unwanted encounters on a regular basis. Because of Alani, they would have to be nice to Mia, even if on the surface.

Open conflict would serve no one well...not Alani and her family, and not her own.

Katie groaned and fell back onto the top of her bed, letting her head sink into the down pillows. She squeezed her eyes tightly against the tears that formed and all that was ahead.

In the many months since her father's death, Katie and her family had worked hard to cling to joy, to focus on the good and not the bad. Proudly, they had been successful. Life was again good.

One diagnosis, and all that had changed.

When it came to the situation with Mia, the Briscoes would be forced to set aside their hurt, deny their own pain, and do what was best for Alani, at least temporarily.

That, she thought, was all her family needed.

Katie wasn't sure how long she'd been asleep when she felt the weight of her husband on the bed beside her. His hand gently brushed aside hair from her face that had been damp with tears and now clung to her cheeks.

"You okay?" Jon whispered.

She nodded.

Jon kissed the top of her head. "Don't worry about Willa. I took care of it. She's grounded, of course. That Devon boy seems like a good kid," he remarked. "They both simply made a bad judgment." Jon chuckled. "But then, most teens do at some point."

"Jon?" she asked.

"Yeah, babe?"

"Do you think he loved her?"

Jon ran his hand along her jawline. "Who"

"Do you think my dad loved Mia?" She paused. "I mean, more than Mom? More than Christel, Shane, Aiden, and me?"

"Love is complicated," Jon murmured. "I'm sure your dad loved his family."

Katie took both hands and rubbed her face. "I just feel like a mess. I hate being a mess."

Jon nodded sympathetically. "Something like what you and your family have gone through," he said, slowly. "It makes you see life through a different lens. You begin to question everything you knew to be true, and wonder if maybe it wasn't."

He drew her into a tight embrace. "I think it's hard not to fall apart, at least a little, when your view of life is shifting."

Jon leaned back and studied her a moment, his warm, brown eyes narrowing to seek out the place where she couldn't hide from him. He picked up her hand and kissed her knuckles. "When the foundation beneath your feet crumbles, the key is to lean on others for stability."

"I'm here, Katie. I won't let you fall."

33

The weeks following Alani's diagnosis and surgery were filled with activity on every front. Alani's oncology team made it clear they wanted to hit this cancer with everything at their disposal. They had to wait for Alani's surgical incisions to heal before they could begin chemotherapy drugs. The drugs were quite toxic and would interfere with the healing process if they started the regimen too soon.

"Chemotherapy can be a bit unpredictable," Dr. Hinske warned. "Initially, we'll want to schedule her treatments on a weekly basis; however, subsequent sessions will depend entirely on her blood count levels. We'll monitor those closely. It's not uncommon to skip a week of treatment occasionally, even more, while we wait for levels to rise."

Alani was released from the hospital and returned to her home in Maui a week after surgery. Mia alerted everyone that she had taken an extended leave of absence from her job and would be staying on island for as long as necessary. She intended to be Alani's primary caretaker, even though the process was expected to take many months.

Despite the past, Ava was grateful Alani's daughter had selflessly stepped up. This freed Ava to return her focus, at least in part, to the golf course renovation.

She had learned in recent weeks that their decision to relocate several of the holes out of potential flood zones would be more costly than originally anticipated. Topography maps obtained from the county were in error and failed to reveal a buried lava flow that crept over the property line. Tom recommended routing the fairways another direction to avoid water pooling beneath the surface which could create issues with the grass.

"What are we looking at?" she asked him when he told her.

Tom shook his head. "I wish I had better news." He handed her a revised budget that was substantially increased from the original.

Ava's eyes flew open. "Oh my. That is different."

"I'm so sorry, Ava. I wish there was something I could do. Unfortunately, we encounter these issues far more often than I like."

Ava attempted a smile. "I appreciate that. I'm so glad you are heading up this renovation, especially since my attention has been pulled away lately."

They walked the golf cart path heading back in the direction of the clubhouse. "How is your friend?"

Ava's throat choked a little as she pushed out the words she still could barely say. "It's cancer, stage IV."

Immediately concern was apparent on Tom's face. "Oh, Ava. No. I'm so sorry."

"We are encouraged with the information we were given by the treatment team. While it would have been much better had the lumps been attended to much earlier, advancements in treatment options provide hope. Breast cancer is not necessarily a death sentence anymore...even at stage IV. The worry, of course, is lymph node involvement and potential spread. Dr.

Hinske and his team have developed an intense treatment program. The months ahead won't be easy for Alani, but my dear friend is tough. Her indubitable spirit, coupled with her faith, will bring her to the finish line."

Tom grew concerned. "But what about you? This must be hard, especially given..." He let his words drift, not voicing the recent loss of her husband.

"I intend to stay busy and keep my mind occupied. I plan on focusing on the positive, the best I'm able. Like Alani told me as we were packing up her things and getting ready to bring her home, 'If you don't like something, change it. If you can't change it, change the way you think about it.' It's one of her favorite quotes, outside the Bible, that is."

"She sounds like a really good person."

"Oh, she is. I would love for you to get to know Alani. You'll be the benefactor of any time spent with her, no doubt."

She smiled. "Once, Alani was excited to take me to a new yogurt shop that opened up in the Shops at Wailea. There were lots of soft-serve choices and even more topping options. They charged by the ounce. We went through the line filling our little dishes. When we got to the counter with all the toppings, Alani leaned and whispered, 'Don't get the M&Ms...too heavy. I have a bag in my purse.'"

They both laughed.

Out of the blue, Ava's emotions took over. She teared up.

Embarrassed, she rubbed the moisture from her eyes. "Sorry, I really do dwell on the positive, but..."

Tom reached for her hand. "But you care deeply about your friend."

She sniffed. "Yes."

He squeezed her hand. "Tell you what, let's practice some of what Alani preaches. Let's get your mind on something else. Let's do something fun. I have been meaning to take an excursion over to Lana'i." Tom swept his arm in the direction of the golf course. "Everything is set for this afternoon. I can slip away. What do you say? Want to go with me?"

Lana'i was the smallest inhabited island in Hawaii. Only nine miles from Maui yet a world away, Lana'i could feel like two places. The first was found in luxurious resorts with world-class amenities and the other was rugged terrain with off-the-beaten-path treasures to explore.

Ava hesitated. She'd already been absent from her duties at Pali Maui for several days in light of Alani's illness. She glanced into Tom's pleading eyes and her resistance faded. "I shouldn't...but, yes. An afternoon trip away might be just the thing I most need. A mental reset." She smiled widely. "And you're in luck. My brother, Jack, runs an excursion company. Perhaps you've heard of him...Captain Jack?"

Tom's eyes widened. "Captain Jack is your brother? No way!"

She grinned and nodded. "Some say we're nothing alike."

Her new friend found that funny. He chuckled. "You don't say." He shook his head. "I spent an evening sitting up to a bar in Lahaina when this big Santa Claus of a man came and plopped down beside me. Over the next few hours, he filled me with whiskey and lots of colorful stories. I can't believe Captain Jack is your brother."

"Jack is much older than me and Vanessa," Ava explained. "He was in high school, well...until he dropped out...when Vanessa and I were still in grade school."

Ava pulled her phone from her pocket. "I'll give Jack a quick call and see if he can make room for us this afternoon."

An hour later, Ava and Tom stood on the waterfront in downtown Lahaina waiting to climb aboard the *Canefire*. The skies overhead were unusually cloudy this afternoon which drove away Jack's normal crowds. Today, Ava and Tom would share the ride with only one other couple, Keith and Sarah

Crouch from Dallas, Texas. They were visiting Maui for their fiftieth wedding anniversary.

"All aboard," Captain Jack called out. He stood on the deck with his tan belly extending out of his unbuttoned Hawaiian print shirt. He wore board shorts and flip-flops with an unlit cigar wedged between his sun-cracked lips. As Sarah stepped up to the side of the boat, Jack extended a hand and helped her into the vessel.

The trip over to Lana'i took just under an hour and was uneventful, save for the fact Jack kept them entertained with more of his stories.

"Bet you didn't know that over 80 percent of this little island is owned by Larry Ellison, founder of Oracle corporation."

He pushed a pair of sunglasses up into his sun-bleached-hair. "You know the difference between God and Larry Ellison?" Without waiting for a reply, he answered his own question. "God doesn't think He's Larry Ellison." He tossed his head back and belly-laughed.

Ava gave him a look, then glanced over at the couple sitting across the boat from them. Both of their eyes were wide with surprise.

Compelled to apologize for her brother's crass sense of humor, Ava stood and offered them a cold drink.

"Uh, that would be nice," Sarah, their fellow boat passenger, said.

Ava retrieved drinks from the onboard cooler and passed them out. As she resumed her seat next to Tom, she leaned to her brother. "You are awful. That's all I have to say."

Jack rubbed his bare belly. "Yet, you love me like a brother."

Ava laughed as she watched the frothy white wake trail behind the boat motor. "That would be true."

The boat slowed as it passed a floating buoy, then drifted to a stop at the shoreline. Jack cut the motor and they disembarked. Tom immediately looked around astounded. "It's more beautiful than the pictures I've seen."

Ava knew what he meant. The locals have an often-used term *ike maka*—to feel the wind of that place, to feel the dirt. Nothing compared to actually experiencing the islands of Hawaii.

They walked ashore past a sign that read "Dolphins Resting in the Bay."

Tom grinned. "That's something you don't see every day."

As if on cue, a small group of people standing several yards from the *Canefire* pointed out into the water. Ava and Tom let their gazes follow and saw a pod of dolphins breaking surface, their bottlenoses high in the hair.

Tom shook his head. "That's just amazing." It's all he could seem to say as he stared, mesmerized.

They headed out on foot from Manele Boat Harbor to Hulupoe Bay Beach. In the distance, they could see Pu'u Pene, also known as Sweetheart Rock, a black outcropping that jutted from the water.

Upon Jack's recommendation, they rented a topless Jeep and went off-roading at the Garden of the Gods. Narrow roads wound through the landscape covered with red dirt and lava rocks. Ava hung onto the roll bar as Tom directed their vehicle through water-filled mudholes, sending drops spraying and landing in Ava's hair.

She laughed and held on tighter.

At the end of one particular trail, Tom pulled the Jeep to a stop. In the far distance, a vista of turquoise-colored water spanned as far as the eye could see. If they looked really hard, Maui could be spotted. Today, it was particularly difficult to make out the bigger island due to the gray clouds that hovered.

Ava trekked to the back of the Jeep and retrieved sandwiches and bottles of beer she'd taken from the stash Jack had on the boat.

Tom and Ava made their way to a large rock with a flattened top and set up a makeshift picnic.

"This has been just what I needed," Ava told him as she unwrapped her turkey sandwich. "I'm having fun."

"Me, too," he wholeheartedly agreed.

Over the next while, they chatted...about everything and nothing. Without the normal pressures of life pushing at them, they simply enjoyed each other's company. The travel brochures were completely accurate...there was no better place to relax than on the tiny island of Lana'i.

"I noticed Mig had a lady friend visiting the other day," Tom mentioned between bites.

Ava nodded. "Oh, yes. My friend appears to be completely infatuated with the island's new realtor. Her name is Wimberly Ann Jenkins. She's not anyone I could ever picture would draw Mig's attention, but I guess you can't plan love."

A small smile, that unbeknownst to her, had been playing on her lips drew him to give her a look, one that was hard to read. "I find myself jealous," he admitted. "It's a valuable thing, finding someone to love."

Ava was instantly surprised at the admission, the longing she heard in his voice. "Yes," she quietly agreed. "It is."

34

On the way back from Lana'i, Captain Jack listened to the radio, gathering reports of an unexpected incoming storm. Out in the ocean during a tropical downpour is not where you want to be. Accordingly, he revved the motor to the highest setting and made haste getting back to Lahaina.

"The good seaman weathers the storm he cannot avoid, and avoids the storm he cannot weather," he said, laughing, and tossed his unlit cigar onto the dash of his vessel.

Upon arrival, the cloud-covered sky opened up and large drops fell to the ground like bullets exploding. Ava and Tom clambered from the boat, quickly hugged Jack goodbye and ran for Tom's car. By the time they arrived at his vehicle, it was pouring.

After helping Ava inside, Tom climbed into the driver's side of his SUV and started the engine. "Whew, that was close!"

Ava laughed and checked her appearance in the mirror on his visor. She looked like a drowned rat. "Maui weather can sure be surprising," she said, brushing her fingers through her hair.

"You can say that again." Tom reached and turned on the radio.

"*Warning. A severe low-pressure system has developed over the archipelago. As a result, a strong storm packing high winds and extremely heavy rain is predicted in the coming hours,*" the reporter announced. "*These conditions could bring a threat of flooding and power outages. Now is the time to make sure you have an emergency plan in place and supplies ready should you need to move away from rising water.*"

Tom frowned. "That doesn't sound good."

Ava joined him in showing concern. "No, it doesn't."

Tom put his SUV in gear and backed out of the parking spot. "I think we'd best skip stopping for dinner and instead get you back to your place."

They'd driven about ten minutes south when the rain poured in earnest, coming down so hard the wipers could barely keep the windshield clear enough to see. Tom slowed.

Suddenly, he threw on the brakes. The motion sent Ava careening forward. Only the seatbelt stopped her from hitting the dashboard. "What the—?" she exclaimed, her hand flying to her chest in surprise.

"Hang on." Tom maneuvered his vehicle to the right to avoid a downed tree that had fallen into his lane.

Ava's worry grew as she saw a long line of cars forming ahead of them.

Maui was susceptible to Kona lows, low-pressure systems that formed and could draw tremendous amounts of tropical moisture from the equatorial regions. Worse, while Kona lows seemed to appear out of nowhere, they tended to move slowly, keeping heavy rain and rare thunder showers focused over the area for a prolonged amount of time. This made the entire island prone to flooding. They could also carry strong, damaging winds.

The traffic was heavy delaying their ability to make much headway.

By the time they hit the entrance to Pali Maui, the wind had picked up. The tops of the palms lining the long lane leading to Ava's house, the office and the packing sheds oscillated in a manner so extreme, the motion sent fronds dropping to the ground. Hibiscus petals littered the muddy surface and pools of water began lining the lane.

"Whew. This looks bad," Tom said as he pushed through puddles filled with muddy water.

Ava was busy on her phone, trying to reach Mig. She sighed when all she got was a busy signal and finally put it away. "Cell service must be very spotty."

At the end of the lane, Tom pulled into the yard, parked, and grabbed an umbrella from the back seat. He got out and moved for the passenger door, holding the umbrella open over Ava's head as she scrambled from the car.

Unfortunately, his chivalry met with resistance. The wind caught the brim of the umbrella crushing the fabric. Annoyed, Tom tossed the now useless thing into his back seat.

Mig rushed to meet them. "I've been trying to reach you," he hollered to Ava over the sound of the wind.

She held up her phone. "Bad service."

"I have things secured. The sheds, the equipment. Sent the workers home over an hour ago. Weather reports warn this will be worse than most."

While the news came as no surprise, Ava's gut pulled in on itself. "This will delay production, no doubt." She didn't want to consider the financial hit they would take as a result.

She turned to Tom. "We should check on the golf course."

"No need," Mig shouted and waved them inside the office to get out of the rain. "I sent some of the boys over. Everything is as secure as possible. We simply have to wait this out."

This was not the first time a storm of this magnitude had rolled through. While not common in Maui, strong storms were possible. Several years ago, an earthen wall of the Kaupakalua Dam in Haiku breached in east Maui amid heavy rains and flooding, prompting authorities to issue an evacuation order for everyone downstream.

At least six homes were damaged or destroyed. There was evidence of landslides as well. Aiden reported the Maui Emergency Services received more than a dozen calls for help from residents who were trapped in their homes because of rising flood waters and mud rushing down a hillside.

"Have you heard from Aiden?" she asked Mig.

He shook his head. "No, but I think it's certain he and his team have their hands full in this mess. Evacuating all the beaches will be a major chore, let alone the traffic accidents and people just being stupid out there, putting themselves and others in danger."

"How about Christel, Shane and Katie?"

Mig ticked off his report. Christel was home with Evan. Shane had picked up Carson from daycare and had arrived home before the worst hit. Katie, Jon and the girls were tucked safely inside their house. "Wimberly Ann is watching the storm reports on my television."

Relieved, Ava pulled Mig into a hug. "Thank you." It went without saying that nothing around here would run properly without her faithful operations manager.

The door flew open and Vanessa rushed inside. With her backside, she struggled and pushed the door closed behind her. "What in the heck? Rain...in Maui? That's not what the travel brochures advertise!"

Vanessa straightened her hair. "I need to speak to Jim and see if he can't pass a law against these kinds of storms. Not only do they wreak havoc on tourism, the wind does a number on this expensive updo." She frowned and looked at

Ava. "Oh, don't give me that look. These loose curls cost me over $200."

When it looked like the storm would continue into the night hours, Ava turned to Tom. "You'll stay in my guestroom." She left no question, no opportunity for him to say no. "It's not safe for you to drive anywhere in this."

The lights flickered and the room suddenly went dark.

They collectively groaned.

"Give me a minute," Mig hollered. He tightened his jacket and headed outside with Tom close on his heels.

Minutes later, the generator outside revved to life. The lights overhead lit back up, though not as bright as normal.

Ava turned to Vanessa. "You might want to plug your phone in now, while you have an opportunity."

Vanessa's expression quickly changed. "Oh, yes. I will." She scurried over and plugged in her cell. "The campaign office might be trying to reach me."

Ava held back from letting her own face show how dim-witted her sister could be sometimes. "No one is at the office, Vanessa. Not in this storm."

"But—"

"She's right," Mig offered as he returned. "People on the island know not to take these storm warnings lightly." He turned to Ava. "That generator should do its job and power things."

"Let's not take chances. We should limit usage. C'mon. Let's head over to the house." Ava told them all. "And Mig...would you call Jon and Katie and have them gather the kids and meet us over there? We can't run power to my house and theirs and still keep the refrigeration units running."

Mig zipped up his jacket. "I think that's a good idea. We also need to reserve enough power to keep the electric fences viable." He shook his head. "We're going to be really glad we invested in that new converter last year."

Vanessa lifted her brows. "You mean you want us to go out in this again?"

Ava gave her sister an exasperated look. "You'll survive, Prissy Miss."

35

They'd only been over at Ava's less than an hour when she glanced out the window and noticed a pair of headlights slowly making their way up the lane. "Who in the world could that be?"

Shortly after the remark left her lips, she noticed a bright yellow emergency services rig pulling into the yard. "It must be Aiden," she said.

The door flew open minutes later and Shane blasted through the door with a heavily-covered bundle in his arms. Aiden followed closely behind. "Hi, Mom. Can't stay but thought it best if Shane and Carson weren't alone in this."

Ava drew her youngest son into her arms and helped him undo the blanket. Soon, a little face appeared with a big smile on his tiny dimpled face. Carson let out a delighted coo and then stuck his thumb in his mouth, completely content and unaware of danger.

Ava pulled Aiden into a grateful hug. "Thank you, son," she said. "I would have worried."

Tom pointed out the window. "Here comes somebody else."

Ava burrowed her brows into a concerned frown. "Who else is out there in this?"

In unison, Katie and Willa answered her. "It's Evan and Christel."

Ava didn't know whether to be extremely happy they would all ride out this storm together, or to feel concerned that her family would take such risks in order to gather. She shook her head. None of that mattered now. What mattered is that everyone was here, and they were all safe.

"I can't stay," Aiden announced. Despite groans of opposition, he gathered a few water bottles from his mother's refrigerator and headed for the door, promising to stay in touch.

"Are you sure you'll be all right?" Wimberly Ann asked, wringing her manicured hands with worry as he closed the door behind him. "It's so dangerous out there."

Mig pulled his girlfriend into a shoulder hug. "He'll be fine, honey. This is what Aiden does."

Ava swept a kiss along her son's cheek on his way out the door. "Please don't take any undue risks."

Katie grabbed Willa by the hand. "What say we divert our attention from what's going on outside? I propose we play a game."

"A game?" her daughter said, looking more than a little skeptical.

"Yeah, a game," Jon said, joining his wife. "Let's play charades!"

Ava was with Willa. She doubted that a simple game would implement any meaningful diversion. Even so, she played along. "I'm in."

Tom nodded. "Count me in."

Wimberly Ann's worried expression brightened. "Oh, that sounds fun."

Mig begged off. "I need to keep an eye for incoming calls," he explained. "Play without me. I'll be the cheerleader."

Shane quickly grabbed his favorite spot on the sofa. "You're on."

They divided up into teams with two captains...Jon and Shane. Evan, Willa, and Ava were on Shane's team. Christel, Katie, and Wimberly Ann were Team Jon. They flipped coins for Vanessa, who ended up with Shane.

"Isn't that unfair?" Willa asked. "I mean, that gives us an advantage."

"Not really," Ava quickly asserted.

Vanessa rolled her eyes and let out a playful huff. "Say what you might but I beg to differ. I am a master at charades." She narrowed her eyes signaling a serious challenge was about to take place. "Game on!"

Vanessa stood. "Me, first." She moved her hands like a camera then lifted four fingers in the air.

"A movie. Four words," Willa shouted.

Vanessa nodded and held up one finger.

"First word," Ava said, a little more sedately than her granddaughter.

Vanessa grinned and waved, then walked away like she was leaving.

"Goodbye," Shane hollered. This caused little Carson's eyes to pop wide open with surprise. They waited for him to cry, but all he did was smile.

Vanessa shook her head, silently urging for them to try again.

It took several more attempts before Vanessa motioned to pass and went on to the second word. She used her thumb and forefinger to indicate it was a short word. Before waiting for a reply, she motioned that the third word was also short.

Ava nodded. "Go on. We'll fill those in."

Vanessa smiled and held up four fingers.

Evan casually put his arm around his wife.

"Hey, no fraternizing with the enemy," Jon said, grinning, but with a resolute look on his face.

Evan dropped his arm. "Gee, sorry. This family takes game night seriously," he murmured.

Vanessa repeated her motion and held up four fingers. Immediately, she acted like she was getting blown by a strong gust. She mimicked being barely able to walk and shielded her face with her arm.

Willa crossed her arms against her chest. "Oh, that's too easy. Wind."

Vanessa nodded wildly and pointed to her niece. Willa had guessed correctly.

Evan leaned forward on his knees, cocked his head and grinned. "*Gone With the Wind.*"

Vanessa couldn't contain her excitement. She jumped up and down. "Yes! That's it!"

Ava looked between Evan and Vanessa. "How in the world did you get that?" She pointed to her sister. "From those clues?"

Evan shrugged. "Just lucky, I guess."

Vanessa blew on her fingernails and shined them on her shirt in victory. "No luck needed. That was an exhibition of pure skill," she taunted. She turned to face her sister. "I repeat... pure skill."

They played like that for over an hour, surprising Ava at how she'd been wrong. The game was serving to keep their minds off the storm after all. She was just about to get up and serve up some snacks when a crash sounded just outside the multi-slide glass doors leading to the lanai and pool area.

They all rushed to the window and Ava flicked on the outside light to discover a tree limb in the pool, along with several pieces of Ava's patio furniture. Leaves and smaller limbs were strewn across the tiles. Beyond the pool area was pitch black. A deep groaning howling sound sent warning that a savage storm continued to rage across the island.

Ava chewed her knuckle. The force of the wind was nothing to fool with. She could only imagine the damage it would leave behind.

Mig tossed his phone to the counter. "Service is gone."

"Maybe we should turn on the television," Christel suggested.

Evan picked up the remote and the television thankfully flickered on. The weatherman looked harried. He ran his hand over the top of his hair as he announced, "*It won't be until morning that we know the extent of this storm and the resulting damage. I think we can safely say the destruction is expected to be extensive.*"

36

By morning, the truth of the weatherman's predictions became apparent.

Power outages and widespread road closures had led to a state of emergency. Conditions across the island had turned extremely treacherous as roadways were washed out, including some of the main highways. Debris and fallen trees joined leaning power poles...all signs this had been no ordinary storm.

Flooding impacted roads and homes across Maui, most particularly near Kihei, eating away portions of the surrounding roads and leaving almost no shoulder past the bridge near the Hawaiian Islands Humpback Whale National Marine Sanctuary.

Hours after the wind calmed and the downpour settled to a light and steady rain, most of the island remained without power. Displaced residents were taken in and Ori's Ka Hale a Ke Ola Resource Center was overflowing.

The most dangerous situations were the multiple mudslides, which caused Ava and Mig great concern as they headed out with the others to assess the impact the storm had on Pali Maui and the surrounding mountainside behind the pineapple plantation.

What they found was gut-wrenching. The ravenous rain and wind had indeed wreaked havoc.

The roof on Na Ka'Oi had sprung a leak. Incoming rain had damaged both the kitchen and the dining area in Jon's restaurant.

A minor mudslide had taken out nearly all of Jon and Katie's landscaping around their newly-built home.

A downed tree had blocked the entrance to the gift shop and another limb had gone through a glass window knocking over a display of pineapple-motif mugs and glassware, shattering most of the pieces.

Strong winds had lifted a sheath of metal from the building where Mig stored his precious Chevy Bel Air and had thrown it into the side of his car. Upon seeing the ugly dent, Mig swallowed back emotion. "It's just a material thing. It can be fixed."

Ava's pool was filled with mud and debris. Her landscaping looked like the Loch Ness monster had strolled through, stopping casually to chomp off the tops off her islands of paradise and her canna lilies. Surrounding plumeria trees were stripped of blooms and mud seeped into the tile grout where her outdoor kitchen was located.

Like Mig said, everything was material and could be replaced and restored. Still, the storm had left an ugly mess. The scene was heartbreaking.

"Oh, Mom," Katie muttered as she surveyed the damage.

Shane shook his head. "Man, who knew wind could do all this?"

An incoming text from Aiden assured Ava he had made it through the emergency unscathed, even if exhausted. There had been car accidents, water rescues and lots of emergency transports to hospitals and the shelter.

More importantly, he'd checked in on Elta and Alani. They

were fine and so was their home, save for some minor things. The Wailea Chapel had somehow escaped suffering any damage...no doubt a result of prayers going up from the congregation.

Tom's golf course project was perhaps the most affected. The fairways were filled with mud and debris. The sand traps were bare of sand. The water hazards filled with muddy water and flooding over. "Insurance will take care of all of this," Tom assured Ava as she fought back tears.

"Insurance won't cover all of the loss," Christel noted, miserably. "There are weather hazard exclusions and a high deductible I don't even want to think about."

Ava drew her oldest daughter's shoulders into a tight hug. "Our upcoming crop will bring some instant cash. It'll be tight, but we'll make it through," she assured, despite her faltering conviction that everything she claimed was true.

It wasn't until hours later that Ava discovered how wrong she'd been when Mig came tearing into the yard on his utility terrain vehicle. He came screeching to a stop and hopped off. "Ava, I have bad news."

Her heart stopped. She waited for his report unable to breathe. "What is it, Mig?"

His face flushed. "The power...the electric fencing shut off."

"And?" Her blood ran cold. She knew, and didn't know, what was coming.

Mig wrung his cap in his hands. "Wild feral pigs got in to the pineapple fields. Destroyed all of the lower fields and wiped out most of our harvest."

In that instant, Ava's world dropped out from underneath her.

37

Ava's hand gripped the steering wheel tightly as she drove along Honoapiilani Highway, taking care to slow for orange cones and emergency vehicles out removing debris from the road. Tears streamed down her face.

From the time she was a little girl, her dad told her she was strong, resilient, and capable. She'd bring home a report card filled with the highest marks and he'd pat her shoulder and tell her he was not surprised. When other girls could barely calculate a 50 percent off sale at their favorite clothing store, she was helping her father prepare financials for tax time. She learned to drive years earlier than any of her friends and could change a tire like any boy. Even as a child, she could cook and clean and do laundry. Growing up, she planted a garden every year, learned to can, and could kill, cut up, and fry a chicken with the best of the islanders.

Boys called, even asked her out on dates. She passed, using the excuse that she didn't have time. Truth was, she was wearing too many hats...none of them meant for a little girl. Like most kids who lost a parent early in life, she had to grow up fast.

As she moved into adulthood, she continued to prove her abilities. She stepped up and took on the fledgling Pali Maui her dad purchased as a tax write-off, turned the operation into one of the most respected pineapple farms in the islands—in the world, for that matter. In the ensuing years, she brokered contracts shoulder-to-shoulder with CEOs and CFOs of some of the most impressive companies in Forbes business magazine. Soon, everyone respected her negotiation acumen and superior head for business.

Don't get her wrong. She'd been blessed beyond measure. She didn't take that lightly.

Yet, the truth was...she'd also weathered much heartache and loss in her fifty-four years. She'd faced fear and struggle, shame and loneliness. The load had been too heavy sometimes, too much.

Now this.

Never had she felt so defeated.

Never had she felt the weight of the world on her shoulders, and the tenuous knowledge that she didn't have the emotional strength to go on. Never had she let herself feel the extent of it all.

Ava took a deep breath and shook her head as she slowed and turned into the entrance to Launiupoko Beach Park. Despite the closed sign, a park worker, who was a former high school friend, waved her on in. "Be careful," he warned. "There's a lot of mud and debris."

She nodded, glad for the solitude, and pulled forward with caution, finding a parking spot that was only partially covered with mud. She maneuvered her car up to the curb and cut the engine, then sat there, not wanting to move.

She needed some time alone, away from eyes seeking reassurance, seeking direction. She couldn't bear to look into Christel's distraught face as the realization sunk in and what the loss of the pineapple harvest meant. They shared the knowledge that this hit could easily take them out financially, or at least wound them for a good long time. Katie's fear was overwhelming, her frantic search for stability. She and Jon had lost their former house to a fire. While the storm didn't severely damage their newly-built home, her carefully planned landscaping was completely destroyed. Windows were broken in the gift shop allowing incoming rain to ruin her merchandise.

Aiden and Shane...well, a mother knew her sons. On the outside, they were tough. Inside, they had melted into puddles, just like their sisters. What would this loss impact them as the viability of their inheritance teetered?

Ava was an optimist. Not everything on the horizon was doom and gloom. Her family would eventually find a way forward. God always provided.

Right now, none of that mattered. The set-back was devastating.

Now, all she wanted to do was sit with herself and wonder why.

She grabbed her jacket and got out of her car, stepping into the warmth of the day. Overhead, clouds still robbed the beaches of sunshine, but the storm had passed and the temperatures were reflective of that.

Ava stepped over the low railing that bordered the parking lot and made the few muddy steps to the paved walking path that led to the sand-filled beach.

Launiupoko Beach was typically crowded with families and tourists—a popular spot to spend the day because of the beautiful views and the calm tidal pools that were ideal for little ones to swim in without fear of waves sweeping them off their feet. This was a spot where many wedding photos were taken with palm trees extending over the water, creating a stunning backdrop, especially when the sun set.

It was a perfect place for Ava to sit and reflect.

She crossed the expanse of sand and found her way to a large piece of driftwood and parked her bottom, filling her lungs with the moist air. The atmosphere remained permeated with the trademark smell of plumeria and tropical scents, but a heaviness also filled the air—a slight earthy smell, like the mud that now covered much of the island.

Tears formed again, burning at her eyes. Despite years of stoic resistance, Ava now felt the ache of her accumulated disappointment...all of it.

Why?

Why had her mother died, leaving her to learn of fashion and hair and monthly periods from books and magazines? Why had Lincoln been so distant, leaving so much on her shoulders? Why had he betrayed her? Why had he died in that accident, leaving her alone to pick up the pieces from a discovery none of them saw coming?

Was there a reason that Alani had cancer? Why her? No one should be more immune from tragedy and hardship than her best friend, who was faithful and generous and always there by her side, no matter what.

The knocks were building up. Ava felt herself toppling over.

With Alani was so very ill and unavailable, who would catch her if she fell?

Ava wanted to hold onto her joy, but admittedly her grip was loosening. Maintaining happiness was getting more and more tenuous.

Despite trying not to, she worried about her kids.

She'd insisted on them leaving the past behind and walking forward into a new beginning after Lincoln died. She'd lifted her arms and held up their family when events threatened to crumble their structure. Somehow, when she needed it most, she'd found the fortitude to be there for each of them through the hurtful shift in their family, the quaking fault line that threatened to make all of them lose their footing.

Ava treasured her own strength...but it came at a cost.

When all you did was give, eventually everything inside became used up and you found yourself depleted.

Ava sniffed loudly, not caring that the sudden noise caused a nearby bird to take flight.

Yes, she was having a pity party. She'd certainly earned one...a morose celebration with champagne and balloons and sadness and regret.

When everything she'd worked so hard to build was threatened, it punctured her soul. Pali Maui was as much a part of her as her own children. They were birthed from her body, Pali Maui was birthed from her passion, her essence.

Tom was correct. Repairs could be made. In time, the damage would be restored.

While insurance was limited to help with recovery, this event had severely injured their cash flow and ability to be feasible. Would they make it out of this? Could they recover?

Ava straightened and lifted her chin. She'd have to find a way to rebuild. If not for her, then for the people she cherished. She had no choice but to push forward, especially given Mig's investment was now at risk, as well as her children's financial future. She'd always planned on passing Pali Maui on...keeping her precious legacy alive by gifting the pineapple operation and associated business ventures on to her children and grandchildren.

Ava angrily wiped at her tears.

Giving up was unthinkable. Yet, the work ahead...she could barely fathom the effort. The thought of what all that meant nearly put her on her knees.

Life could be so unfair.

And then it happened again. The emotional wave pulled her back out to sea.

Ava buried her hands in her face and let herself cry. She needed it. Needed to cleanse herself of this overwhelming emotion. She would never find joy again until she ridded herself of this despair.

"Mom?"

Ava sniffed and wiped her face with the sleeve of her jacket. She turned toward the voice to see a small group walking toward her.

As they neared, their identities became clear: Christel, Aiden, Shane, and Katie.

Funny...a deep sense of peace immediately blanketed her.

As her children reached her side, they immediately enfolded her into their arms. Their shared strength filled her... those empty places deep within. In a crazy twist, they were here for her. They were holding her up. She was not alone.

Aiden was the first to speak. "Mom, are you afraid?"

And there the question hung, the one she most dreaded. She'd never really admitted her fears to the people she loved, especially not her children.

Ava took a deep, brave breath. "Yes, of course I'm afraid. Only a fool wouldn't recognize the peril this storm has placed on Pali Maui and our financial situation," she quietly admitted.

Shane leaned his head against her back. "No amount of holding on to the dream is going to keep things from changing, Mom. Sometimes life just hands you...stuff."

Ava couldn't help but smile to herself. Yes, he would know that.

Katie stroked her mother's hair. "Mom, we know how rough Alani's illness has been on you, especially on the heels of last year and losing dad...and all." She let her voice fade slightly at the inference to her father's adultery.

Aiden entwined his fingers in her own. "Mom, we're here for you. You do not face this on your own."

Christel nodded. "We're in this together."

Ava smiled as best she could, trying to record the details of this extraordinary moment in her mind.

She'd been wrong to think the road ahead would be primarily a solo journey. She had the support of these four wonderful human beings...people she had helped fashion into compassionate, caring, smart, and funny folks who she could count on at every turn.

She sniffed.

Even though her best friend remained in treatment and recuperating, Ava still had Alani. No doubt, the woman had her head pressed against the pillow and was praying for her even now. As was Elta and Ori...possibly even Mia, who was showing remorse for what she had done.

There was Mig, her trusted friend and work partner who had helped her build Pali Maui in every way. When it counted, he'd even granted his own finances in support.

Then there was Tom...a new friend. A man she suspected could eventually become more than a passing acquaintance—if, and when, she was ever ready to open her heart again.

The sun suddenly peeked from behind the clouds. The warmth of the sun on her shoulders felt like her own mother, and father, now gazing down from heaven, telling her, *"We've been here, too...never as far as you might have thought."*

Even Lincoln. He'd reminded her that if an accident robbed her of the rest of her life like it had his, her fifty-four years on earth had been enough. They had been full of love.

She'd had the good fortune of many chances to fail and succeed, more love to give and receive—more joy than she could possibly hold. Not because of circumstances, but because of who she traveled this earth with—her friends and family. Her loved ones.

While Ava didn't know what the future held, because of those surrounding her, she would move forward. She would find joy again.

In the distance, an ocean wave hit shore with a familiar sound that lulled her into believing everything would work out.

The Briscoes were survivors.

With a smile firmly planted, Ava would look to the future and find out just what was next.

AFTERWORD

Aloha! Captain Jack here. As you can see, my sister and her family have weathered more storms lately...both literally and figuratively. Ava is a tough cookie, but even the strongest of us can break sometimes. Right?

Those kids of hers, my nieces and nephews...well, they sure came through in that final chapter, didn't they? Christel, Aiden, Katie and Shane are committed to helping their mother pick up the pieces and rebuild. Tom Strobe might just provide a bit of assistance as well. We can all guess what might be coming. Will he help mend my sister's broken heart?

Folks, before I go, I had a chat with Kellie (the author) the other day. Know what she told me? She says she's been getting loads of emails from all of you readers telling her you are loving the Maui Island Series and begging for more stories. Given that, she has decided not to wrap up the series with these four books. You'll be glad to learn that four more books are now on the horizon: *Ohana Sunrise, Sweet Plumeria Dawn, Where Hibiscus Bloom,* and *Songs of the Rainbow.*

Want to see the new covers? Hop on over to Kellie's website

and take a peek. While you're there, don't forget to get yourself a copy of *Ohana Sunrise*, the next book in the series.

'Ole Captain Jack got his copy and I plan to bury my nose in those pages at first chance. For now, I've got to get back to the dock. A group of tourists are anxious to board the *Canefire* and get a look at some whales. The humpbacks have been breeching like crazy this week. These majestic mammals come to our island waters every year to make their babies and they are having a "whale" of a time right now, know what I mean?

Oh, c'mon. Don't go getting all prudish. Here's where you picture me laughing as I rub my belly and chew on my cigar. *winks*

Anyway, grab your coconut bra and grass skirt and hula on over and get a copy of Ohana Sunrise. I'll catch you later. Aloha!

YES, I WANT A COPY OF THE NEXT BOOK!

ACKNOWLEDGMENTS

A special word of thanks to the folks at Maui Pineapple Plantation (waving to Debbie, Lacey, Mary and Ken!) These fine folks let me hang with them and see how pineapples are planted, grown and harvested.

Did you know pineapple crowns are planted in the earth by hand? The pineapples then take fourteen to fifteen months to grow. Maui is known for wild pigs and if they break through the fencing, they can eat a football field worth of produce in no time.

The Maui Pineapples are picked to order and are the sweetest treat you'll ever pop in your mouth...no, really! I had such a fun time on the tour and learned so much. You guys were so supportive of this series and my heart is filled with gratitude.

Thanks also to Elizabeth Mackey for the fabulous cover designs, to Jones House Creative for my web design, to Samantha Hanni of A Word in Season and the rest of my editors, proofreaders and my publishing team. Special thanks to my personal assistant, Danielle Woods. You guys all make this business so much easier, and definitely more fun!

Hugs and a lot of gratitude to my best-selling author friend and critique partner, Jodi Vaughn, who made this book so much better.

To all the readers who hang with me at She's Reading, you are a blast! I can't believe how much fun it is to do those live author chats and introduce you to my author buddies.

Finally, thanks to my readers. All this is for you!

~Kellie

A SNEAK PEEK - OHANA SUNRISE (MAUI ISLAND SERIES BOOK 5)

Chapter 1

In the mornings, after straightening her bed and taking a quick shower, Ava liked to take her cup of hot coffee out onto the lanai where she'd sit and watch the sun rise. She loved how, in those quiet hours of early morning, the horizon would turn lavender, then pink and then turn a light apricot color.

She loved the faint smell of plumeria, pineapple and eucalyptus and the cheerful chorus of Apapane and I'iwi birds, the softness of morning before the day began with all of its demands.

Lately, her interludes had been abruptly cut with the arrival of slow-moving machinery and the loud grinding of diesel motors, followed by booming shouts of workers yelling instructions over the sound of the gears grinding and equipment chugging across the grounds of Pali Maui, her beloved pineapple plantation.

Not that she was complaining. She was more than thankful for the activity.

It had been a little over two months since the big storm that had blown across Maui, creating chaos and damage across the island. Pali Maui had taken a severe hit with downed trees and flooding. Landscaping had to be replaced. Jon's restaurant roof had to be replaced and the interior damage restored. Likewise, the offices and the giftshop needed restoration. The golf course renovation had been markedly hindered. The progress Tom Strobe and his crew had made was essentially obliterated by flooding water. The entire design process had to start over, taking into account the altered terrain. It would now be months before the project would turn any sort of profit.

Worse, a power outage had allowed feral pigs to breech their electric fencing. In a matter of hours, the native boars had consumed a huge portion of the pineapple fields and their harvest had been obliterated.

To say Pali Maui had a financial problem was an understatement.

Ava went to sleep each night and woke each morning thinking about ways to tighten their monetary belts until cash flow could be restored to a healthy level. It had taken some financial gymnastics to keep Pali Maui afloat. For now, they had the resources to move forward, thanks to each one of them liquidating assets and bolstering their balance sheet, including her brother, Jack.

Currently, they were on a narrow footbridge. Any misstep would send the entire operation plummeting into the chasm of bankruptcy and the need to liquidate to meet their obligations, essentially closing down Pali Maui.

Attorneys and financial advisors, including her daughter, Christel, advised chapter eleven bankruptcy, where the court forced debtors to discount what was owed in order to help restructure liabilities, might be an option. Truth was, Ava didn't want to go there. Not if she didn't have to. She always paid her bills in full and on time. That was not going to change as long as she had any say in the matter.

Tom Strobe had graciously offered to discount his contract fee. She'd firmly resisted and declined the proposal. For many reasons...the least of which was her firm belief that a good business owner did not mix business with personal friendships. Doing so only invited issues.

Tom argued when she had explained her position. Even so, she stuck to her guns. Just because she'd run into some cash flow issues did not negate the wisdom of maintaining strong boundaries in the matter. Besides, the forced delays had already impacted Tom and his business, causing the need to reassess his schedule. She's overheard him on a call the other day explaining to a potential client that he could not accept new commitments right now. When he hung up, she urged him to terminate his obligations to her. He wouldn't hear of it. "I'm here and will see this through, Ava. It's important to me."

She and Tom had easily formed a friendship, one she greatly appreciated. Truth was, she saw something in his eyes that suggested he might want more.

The idea that he was attracted to her was flattering.

Tom Strobe was definitely appealing. Despite his strong profile with a solid square face, straight nose and chiseled features, there was a warmth to his face. His blue eyes seemed to see things others missed. He was kind, thoughtful, and generous. They shared deep discussions about literature, music and art, World War II trivia, American history and the future of politics and its effect on the commodities market...and of course, they both loved to discuss golf.

Amend that to mean they *argued* about golf. Tom was adamant that Tiger Woods would make another comeback and top the leader boards again. She'd laughed at the idea. "Nah, he's over. Not only is Tiger physically challenged by compounded injuries, but his bad choices and actions have robbed him of public favor. His mental game is in the sand pit."

Remembering all that made her smile, even now.

Ava had only been single a little over a year. If she wasn't still feeling vacant inside, Tom would definitely be tempting. She should be thrilled that a man like Tom was interested in her, because, clearly, he was. But, instead she was sad.

She would never admit this to anyone, but in the deepest part of her, she carried a secret. Ava knew she was empty and had nothing to give. Lincoln's death and infidelity, coupled with Alana's illness and the losses at Pali Maui...well, it was all too much.

While not a breakdown in the clinical sense, that day on the beach had scared her. She'd felt a darkness that was foreign and alarming. Her emotions were vulnerable. She'd slipped into someone she didn't even recognize. No longer was she the woman in control, the woman who had it all together and was there for everyone. Suddenly, she felt like a wounded puppy and cowered at the notion of experiencing anything hurtful.

Relationships could be sticky...even risky. What if things didn't work out with Tom like hoped? Opening up to another gut-punch might take her under. She might not survive another hit.

Besides, Tom deserved much more than a woman who was romantically hollow.

Ava lifted her chin and stood, gathering her coffee mug. She turned for the house knowing that no matter what Tom's intentions might be, she just couldn't go there.

***

Christel stepped from the shower and reached for the towel. Evan, who was standing at the mirror shaving, dropped his razor and plucked the thick bath sheet from the rack and wrapped it around her torso.

"If I didn't have surgery in an hour, I'd scoop up my wife and return to bed," he taunted.

She grinned back at him. "I wonder if Mrs. Peabody knows she's messing with our sex life?" she quickly said in retort. "But far be it from me to keep my former school teacher in pain."

It was a slight joke between them that Mrs. Peabody's ailments paid for his entire malpractice bill. She had a hip replacement, a knee replacement, and now, she complained her ankle was going out. After delivering dozens of steroid shots to alleviate the pain and swelling, Evan had finally determined an ankle fusion was in order. This morning, he would use screws and plates to internally fixate her bones. Mind you, Christel had not learned this confidential patient information from her husband, but from Mrs. Peabody who kept her hostage in the grocery line last week.

Evan laughed and leaned in and nuzzled her neck. "Raincheck?" he offered.

Christel let herself smile. "It's a date."

She got dressed while he finished shaving. When he gave her another kiss and bid her goodbye, she pasted a smile and told him she'd see him that evening.

As soon as she knew he was gone, she opened her bathroom drawer and withdrew the box, one of three remaining. Using her fingernail, she carefully lifted the glued flap on the end of the long thin box and slid the test stick from its cellophane packaging.

Christel grinned. She didn't need to read the instructions. This wasn't the first test. In fact, it was her third. She only hoped this would not be her third disappointment.

Buoyed with optimism, Christel followed the directions, already anticipating exactly how she might break the good news to Evan. Months back, when he'd first disclosed that he wanted to start a family, she'd initially been reluctant...and more than a little surprised. She shouldn't have been shocked, she supposed. Evan lost his fiancé in a military helicopter accident in Marseilles. Beyond mourning the loss of Tess, he had to let go of plans for a family.

She, too, had been forced to push pause on the idea of children. Jay's addiction had put everything on hold. There was no way she could take on the responsibility of caring for babies while managing her former husband's behavior. It'd taken a lot of counseling and personal reflection to realize she had to release her efforts and let Jay go. Her own sanity required such a painful decision.

Her marriage to Evan had provided a fresh start...and new hope on many fronts. After so much heartache and disappointment, they had both earned some good news.

She pulled the tiny white plastic wand up where she had a clear view of the tiny result window and held her breath while searching for the tell-tale pink line.

Her heart sunk when she found none.

Perhaps she'd done the test wrong, she told herself. She grabbed the handle and opened the bathroom drawer open and pulled another test out. Over the course of the next minutes, she repeated the process.

While she waited the requisite time, her mind rehearsed all she'd been through over the past weeks. The storm and its impact on Pali Maui had buried her under a burden that only she truly understood. She was the chief financial officer. Her family depended on her legal and accounting knowledge to maneuver them through this mess. But what was she to do? Could she make it rain money?

Christel took a deep breath and drew the wand up. She opened her eyes.

Again...nothing.

Unbid tears formed. Her heart sunk.

She'd have to let Evan down again.

ALSO BY KELLIE COATES GILBERT

THE MAUI ISLAND SERIES
Under The Maui Sky

Silver Island Moon

Tides of Paradise

The Last Aloha

Ohana Sunrise

THE PACIFIC BAY SERIES
Chances Are

Remember Us

Chasing Wind

Between Rains

THE SUN VALLEY SERIES
Sisters

Heartbeats

Changes

Promises

LOVE ON VACATION SERIES
Otherwise Engaged

All Fore Love

TEXAS GOLD SERIES
A Woman of Fortune

Where Rivers Part

A Reason to Stay

What Matters Most

STAND ALONE NOVELS

Mother of Pearl

Available at all retailers

www.kelliecoatesgilbert.com

Made in the USA
Middletown, DE
08 February 2024